NESA MILLER

CONTENTS

A GIRL RUNS

Blood stained the night with its rich, dark hue and tainted the air with its metallic stench. The steel of a sweeping blade flashed in the car headlights, blinding her for a moment. She raised her hand to block the glare but wished she had instead ducked behind the front seat and covered her ears, her mother's screams piercing the night. The blood of her parents sprayed across the hood of the car and dotted the windshield as they reached for one another, their bodies sliding apart in pieces before death separated them forever.

Fixated on the gore; she froze.

Her big brother dragged her from the car's back seat. "Look at *me!*" He squeezed her arms until she turned her head and stared into his green eyes. "*Run!*"

Too scared to argue or even think, she ran.

The dark didn't matter. Neither did the rain. Her only thought was to get as far away from the horror as fast as possible. She dared a glance over her shoulder and saw her brother coming round the car. It gave her the courage to dash across the road and dive into a tangled mass of shrubs. Between the tears and the darkness, she could hardly see the branches slapping her face and yanking her hair.

The earth shook beneath her. Frantically pushing the hair from her face, she caught the red glow of two beady eyes followed by the rasp of foul breath. The combination amplified an indescribable stink. Her brother was nowhere to be seen but his command blazed through her mind. *Run!* The stupid shoes she'd worn made it impossible to get traction on the rain-slicked ground. *Man, why didn't I wear my boots?*

The brutal darkness grew claws of its own as she struggled to get out of the shrubs, ripping her dress. She'd chosen it because of the daisy print, her favorite flower, and the style made her feel older, even though her brother said she looked more like twelve than fourteen. It didn't matter what he said. The smile on her dad's face made it worthwhile. Not that she would have admitted it to anyone, especially her mom, who constantly nagged about her usual jeans and T-shirt.

Jeans would've been the better choice tonight. The scratches on her legs stung and the lines of blood tickled. Whatever lay ahead scared the hell out of her, but it had to be better than what pursued her.

Freed from the shrubs, she lost a shoe, kicked off the other, and burst from the trees into the city lights. The wet, empty streets reflected the monotonous red, yellow, green flickers of traffic lights. No less alien, but she could see.

Where did everyone go? It was busy when we went to supper.

A muffled step on wet earth transitioned to a firm stride on solid asphalt. Whatever it was had caught up to her.

Holy shit! Oh. Damn. Sorry, Mom.

The reality of the night sank in.

Mom. Gone forever. Dad.

Stop it! Get a grip, Etain.

She needed to hide, give herself time to think, and come up with a plan. *Plan? Plan what?* A black alley seemed perfect until the disgusting smell of a trash bin hit her in the face. *Ugh.* Breathing through her mouth, she pulled the neckline of her dress over her nose. The fabric filtered the air somewhat but restricted her ability to look over her shoulder. And she had to look. She had to make sure the red-eyed devil hadn't followed her. Distracted by her efforts, the dork in her walked straight into a brick wall.

"Oof..."

Flat on her back, she shivered despite the warmth rising from the asphalt. The thud of his footsteps killed her desire to cry. She clamped a hand over her mouth to make sure no sound escaped.

A man's voice spoke to her—in her head. His manner of speaking told her he wasn't what hunted her. He sounded kind and gentle, and his speech was formal as though he was from a different time. Way too fancy for a red-eyed monster. He urged her to breathe and calm her heart.

"You must move, little one. The shadows will prove a safe haven."

He was right, but fear had her in its grip. She couldn't move. Then came her brother's voice. *"Don't worry about it, little bit. I guess wimping out's your right, being the baby of the family."* And he laughed.

I'll show you what a baby can do.

Despite the shivers, she rolled onto her side, pushed up onto hands and knees, and crawled into a dark doorway.

Heavy steps rumbled past.

The dark figure reeked worse than the trash and growled strange words she didn't understand but the tone left no doubt of their intent. She hugged her knees to her chest, eyes squeezed shut, held her breath, and waited for the touch of smelly fingers. Between the drum of her heart and the smell of her sweat, it was only a matter of time before he found her.

The night was quiet. No monster feet shook the ground. No raspy wheeze contaminated the air. The warm breath she'd been holding whooshed out. "Holy shit." Sucking in a lungful of air, there was a lingering stench, but it was lighter than before. She laid her head back against the brick wall and released the tension she'd held onto since the nightmare had started. Reality soon crept in and hit hard. Tremors shook her to the core. Hot tears flowed down her cheeks, mourning the loss of her family—her mom, her dad, and her brother.

Why? Why my family? What purpose did their deaths serve? She prayed the soothing voice would return and tell her what to do. *Where are you angel?*

As if in answer, a soft glow filled the alley. She wiped her tears and peered around the corner of the doorway. A bright orb glowed, suspended just above the ground. Its silver light sparkled and danced, inviting her to come closer.

Crouched beside the orb, images of home drifted through her mind. A home where the love of her family protected her from the wiles of the world. The warm silver blaze enveloped her. Bit by bit, her fear faded, replaced by a sense of purpose and the knowledge her life would never be the same.

The mud and muck lifted from her skin. Power pulsed through her awkward limbs as her girlish figure transformed into womanly curves and stretched to new heights. The ruined dress fell away, replaced by black leather that fit like a second skin and knee-high black lace up boots with rubber soles to die for.

As she stood, movement from the corner of her eye made her drop into a crouch, afraid of the monster's return. *Please don't see me.* She peered over one shoulder and the other. Nothing sounded in the alleyway. Assured she was alone, she came to her feet and caught her reflection in a windowpane. A nervous laugh slipped out. *You're such a goober, Etain.*

The orb hovered above her head, casting a shimmery light. "Is that me?" Her fingers traced the outline of the woman she'd become, marvelling at the contrast of silver hair against black leather. Leather accentuating an audacious body.

I have boobs. Delighted by the prospect, a new thought came to her. *Could Dad's stories of the Alamir be true?* Tales spoken only when her mom wasn't around. Stories of warriors who lived in the dimension between humans and demons—and worse. *I wonder if what pursued me was the "worse."*

The orb quietly burst and showered her with sparkling stars. She smiled, something she thought she would never do again but soon faded at the realization of what lay ahead.

Would the nightmare evaporate by morning? If it turned out to be real, could she do what was required of an Alamir? *I'm not ready. I'm not prepared.* But revenge burned in her heart and strengthened her resolve. *With or without my angel, I will learn how to fight.*

My family will be avenged.

DON'T LOOK BACK

E tain lifted a hand shielding her eyes from the bright sunshine as she stepped from the dark alley. The cobbled road lined with small shops on either side reminded her of medieval towns she'd seen at the annual Renaissance Faire.

Mom had loved the faire and made sure they each had an appropriate outfit every year. Dad was the king, of course, and Mom was the queen, which made Etain the princess. Her brother refused to be a prince and instead dressed as a medieval-style ninja. He called himself an assassin. *Boys.*

Back when I had a family.

When I was fourteen.

Before the boobs and the second-skin leather with boots that should one want to stomp someone or something into next week most certainly would.

How long ago was it? An hour? Minutes? Ages?

She shivered, dragging a hand through her hair. It had been a warm summer night in Texas. But here, the air nipped at her skin through the leather. Wherever here was.

Some shop signs were in English, some were in a language she didn't recognize, and some had both. The shop where she stood displayed one such sign—*Apothecari. Easy.* One across the road read—*Argraffydd. Whatever that is.* She leaned against the wall of the apothecary and forced herself to take a deep breath.

Dad never mentioned going to another time. What if they don't speak English? She rolled her eyes. *Most of the signs are in English, Etain. They speak English.*

People walked along stone walkways instead of the concrete sidewalks like in her town. She trailed a hand along the stone and wooden facades of the buildings placing one foot in front of the other to keep her balance. It would take time to get used to her new height and body shape.

An occasional head turned her way, but for the most part, no one noticed the silver haired, black-leathered young woman. Why would they? The majority of those she passed also wore leather.

For all the old-world appearance of the shops, their interiors were modern and powered with electricity. Everything a person could want was represented—butcher, bakery, fruit and vegetable market, a small convenience shop, salon, and barber. Whether it was the Alamir realm or not, at least she wouldn't starve or be the victim of bad hair.

Superheroes with super hair. She laughed but frowned with a sigh. *Do they use money? Trade? Whatever it is, I got nothing.*

The chiming of a clock atop a large stone building made her look up. *Noon.* Curiosity drew her toward the town center but a small park with a circular bandstand proved more inviting. After a walk along the cobbled pathways, she noticed a well-used signboard on the side of the bandstand filled with announcements for the town of St. Clears. *Never heard of it.* A piece of paper barely attached flapped in the wind. She traced a finger along the edge of a red dragon imprinted on the corkboard.

School mascot?

The flapping advertisement invited anyone interested in joining a clan to meet at the town hall, food and drink included.

A clan? Definitely Alamir.

Her tummy grumbled at the thought of food but the time on the sheet told her she had a few hours before the meeting. She tugged the paper from the board, folded it neatly, and tucked it into a front pocket of her shirt. Not knowing the day and with no date on the sheet, she hoped it would be tonight.

Etain spent her time getting acquainted with the town. According to the town hall, she'd landed in the Welsh sector in the county of Carmarthenshire. The red dragon was the official emblem of the sector.

The small market down the street offered samples of various fruits and the bakery had samples of breads and pastries. Not enough to fully satisfy but it might hold her over until the meeting.

In the hour right before, she found a public toilet to freshen up and spent the time left sitting in the park until the sun sat low in the sky and the clock struck the hour. She crossed the road and walked up the long stairway to the town hall front doors. A flurry of activity in the foyer lifted her spirits. She was in the right place at the right time.

People dressed in unusual outfits filled the large meeting room, some elaborate, some questionable, and some way too suggestive. It was like being at a comic con without the collectibles and celebrity guests. Although, there were a couple of weapon displays. *I wonder if they're real.*

She went table to table, smiling and giving what she hoped were intelligent answers. If anything, they were honest.

"Where you from?"

"Texas."

"How long have you been Alamir?"

"Uh, well, what time is it?"

Her no-nonsense gaze met one of cool detachment.

"Age?"

She bit her bottom lip and glanced at the people who stood on either side of her.

"How old are you?"

After a sigh, she said, "Fourteen."

Etain suffered a doubtful perusal from head to toe.

"Powers?"

Would empath work? She shrugged.

"Weapons?"

"Are you offering?"

A sardonic smile pre-empted any need for further comment. "Next."

Etain rolled her eyes and made a mental note to adjust her age to... She looked down her front. *Seventeen? Nineteen? Maybe 514 would work? A timeless witch come to cast her magic over the evil doers. I can find a large stick and call it my magical staff. Or is that a wizard?*

After hitting every table in the room, twelve to be exact, she walked out of the hall without a glimmer of an invitation and hadn't had the gumption to approach either of the weapons tables. On the front steps, she watched others disperse in different directions.

Great. Now what? Maybe someone inside can tell me if there's a place I can stay.

She returned to the front doors. Locked. *What? Damn!* She peered through the glass. *Seriously?* As the thoughts passed through her mind, the lights turned off.

She slammed a hand against the door, eyes darting left and right, breath steaming the glass. "Wait a minute! I don't have anywhere to go. Hey! Come back!" No amount of tapping or smacking of the glass brought a response. She turned around and stared into space, not really seeing anything, when a new idea struck. "If they aren't coming out the front door..."

Het boots barely touched the concrete steps in her mad dash to the bottom. A quick turn took her toward the rear of the huge building. *No doors on this side. Maybe there's a back entrance?*

She whipped round the corner and stopped. It was much darker there. Conscious she was alone, Etain kept a keen eye for anything suspicious as she roamed along the wall in search of a door. One appeared midway through her investigation. A lonely, pathetic gray thing with a dinky light above.

Hmm, I guess I can't blame 'em for getting out so quickly. It's creepy back here.

Nonetheless, she tried the handle. *Better inside than out.* Locked. She turned and noticed the park across the street. There were a few streetlamps, but the shadows outnumbered the light. Her mind went to the park at home where she'd seen people asleep on park benches. Sudden tears burned in her eyes. "I'm not a bum."

Then came the rain. "Great." Hands on hips, she lifted her face to the dark skies. "Welcome to the Alamir, loser, where your every nightmare can come true."

She returned to the front, taking her time walking up the stairs to the portico. A glance wrote off the left side. No cubby holes to curl into. It was dark to her right, but she saw the potential. Protection from the rain and prying eyes. The smell wasn't so great but with her options on the slim-to-nothing scale she squeezed into the enclosure, shivering from the cold stone against her backside.

As a distraction, she pulled a nibble from between her breasts. "At least the boobs come in handy." She'd stuffed as many of the little hors d'oeuvres down her top as space and time would allow, plus a bottle of water. Who knew how long it would take to find a clan?

The distraction didn't last long. Images of the previous night crept in, the dark mass blocking the road and Dad getting out of the car despite Mom's protests.

"James, get back in the car. Let's go home. Please."

Her mother, sitting in the front seat, turned to her in the back seat. *She recognized the expression on my face. She knew it was bad. Oh, man! Mom. Dad.*

Tears streamed down her face.

What happened to Robert? He was on his way. I guess they killed him, too.

She wanted to hit something, bash it until it crumbled, and stomp the pieces into oblivion. She bit her bottom lip to keep from screaming and slapped the stone wall beside her. *Why?* Again and again, harder and harder, until the pain in her hand surpassed the anguish in her heart.

They. Did. Not. Deserve. To. Die. To be cut into pieces. I can't stand it! She jammed both hands into her hair. *Please let me die right here, right now. I don't belong here. I want my family.*

When she slammed her hand against the stone again, a flash of blue light made her stop and sit up. "What was that?"

Etain shifted onto her knees and peered over the wall behind her. The town was dark. No blue lights showed anywhere. She settled back into her cubby. "Probably a brain aneurysm about to burst. Good. I hate this place."

EINSTEIN'S LACK OF SENSITIVITY

G rissom circled the autopsy slab, contemplating the female body in front of him. Just as the camera zoomed in it diverted to a Great Dane, walking into the room on its hind legs.

"Rany rireas?"

"Scoob, thanks for coming so quickly. My initial observation would be hypothermia."

Scooby shivered from head to tail. "Rit's rold."

The two leaned over the body as the camera zoomed in again.

Etain jerked awake and blinked several times. She pushed away from the stone wall where her cheek had rested, wiping the drool from her chin.

"You shouldn't be here."

A young man's voice made her jerk again. Not fully awake, she squinted in his general direction.

"Well, I don't wanna be here, so we're even."

"I mean here on the portico," said the light-haired young man. "If you get caught, it could mean trouble."

"It can't be any worse than what I already have." She placed her hands behind her and pushed up onto her feet.

"You're a newbie, aren't you?"

She eyed him for a moment. "Wow. And you must be Einstein."

He chuckled and shifted on his feet. "A comedian. We could use a few more like you."

"I wouldn't wish this on anyone."

"Bad night?"

Etain tilted her head toward her sleeping accommodations. "What do *you* think?" She grabbed her half bottle of water and brushed past the nosey Alamir. "I have to pee."

"There's a public toilet—"

"Yeah, I know. Down the street."

"Don't come back here."

The *pre*-Alamir Etain would have walked away without incident, disappeared, never to be seen again. As she descended the steps, she raised a hand.

But this was *the* Alamir Etain. Instead of a hand wave, she shot him a single finger salute and kept on walking. "Got it, asshole."

If he comes, I'll use a move Robert taught me and beat him with both fists until he cries like a baby.

The hairs on the back of her neck rose as she walked down the street, her body relaxed but ready to react should the idiot come after her.

Any minute now.

There were no footsteps. No hot breath against her neck. No fingertips brushed across her back as she walked into the Ladies. After a quick search of the stalls, she chose the one she'd used the day before, slammed the door, and turned the lock. With a step up onto the toilet, she held her breath. Just in case.

Assured she was alone, her emotions burst free in a mix of relief, uncertainty, and pride. *I flipped him off! And called him an asshole.* A nervous smile touched her lips as she ran a hand through her hair, tears in her eyes, and envisioned a fist bump with her brother. *I actually did it. You'd be proud.*

But a couple of uninvited hoodlums, anger and frustration, crashed the party. *What a jerk. Where does he expect me to go?* She stepped down from the toilet. "What a fucked-up place!" She hit the metal wall to her left. "How am I supposed to learn anything if no one will help me?" She hit the metal wall to her right. "I hate this place. I hate it!"

She pummelled the door with both fists and kept punching long after her anger and frustration were exhausted. The blue lights flashing each time a fist connected with the metal pre-empted the pain and blood. With a final body slam, the hinges screeched as the door came loose and flew across the room into the stalls on the other side. Etain stumbled after it but caught herself at the sinks in the center, panting, her mind spinning. The smell of food cooking made her mouth water.

A movement from the corner of her eye made her turn. In the full-length mirror stood a wild-haired, blood-spattered vigilante encased from head to toe in blue sparks of electrical charges. She walked to the mirror and reached out but quickly pulled her hand back.

A noise from outside served as a reminder of her circumstances. She dashed into another stall, turned the lock, and closed her eyes. Her bloody knuckles ached and her head hurt. But in a crazy way, she felt better, except for the need to pee. Once her stomach stopped churning, she opened one eye at a time and checked out her frame. No more blue light.

Done with her business, she left the stall and washed her hands. The sting of the water on her knuckles made her wince but the splashes against her face were refreshing. It was then she remembered the goodies stuffed in her top. "Bummer." Her light show had fried everything to a crisp.

As she turned off the tap, a young woman walked in and gave her a tentative smile as she passed. At the battered stall, her eyes widened. Etain shrugged. "Some people have no respect."

Back on the street, she turned toward the alley where her journey had begun. *Maybe something will tell me how to get home.* She walked the entire length of the cobbled road, and should she be mistaken on which side of the street she'd been on the day before; she walked down the other side. There were passageways and alleys but none as deep and dark as the one she'd come from.

"Now what?" At the grumble in her stomach, she eyed the small market across the street. *Maybe they have more samples.*

With her first step, she froze. From the direction of the town hall came the snooty, light-haired guy from earlier, and he wasn't alone. His gaze landed on her at the same time she noticed him. He nudged one of his buddies. Payback time.

Big, fat chicken.

She pivoted into a run and ducked into the first passageway running straight through to the next street. Part way up the road, three boys came from around the corner. What were the chances? When they headed in her direction, she checked over her shoulder. A couple more popped out of the passageway. *Shit!*

Etain darted across the street into a small butcher's shop, dashed around the counter, and into the back.

She heard one laugh. "What was that?"

"I told you about leaving the front door open. It invites all kinds of trouble."

"Me business has improved though. People feel welcome."

"Ho! Hold up there, young 'uns."

A scuffle in the shop told her the boys were hot on her ass.

Luckily, the butcher and his assistant executed an excellent interception, giving her time to escape.

Along her way, she passed an array of knives displayed on a wall. A niggle in her gut made her stop. She backed up, eyed the assortment of sharp instruments, and grabbed one she thought would fit her hand. The wooden handle was cool against her palm and had a good feel, not too light, not too heavy, as though it was made for her. She slipped the knife into her boot and scrambled out the back.

An open door across the road gave her another passageway. Which way would they expect her to go? In her experience with boys, they seemed to think girls took the easy route. A quick glance at the slate-tiled rooftops knocked them out as a way of escape. There was no way she'd be able to keep her footing. *But it would be cool.*

Spurred on by the noises from the butcher's shop, she turned right and ran like hell, doubling back toward the main street. She couldn't return to the town hall, but the market and bakery should be safe.

People walked on either side of the street, a few dressed in their superhero choice of attire, but most were in regular street clothes from varying decades. *Centuries,* she corrected in her head as a couple decked out in full Steampunk regalia strolled past. She tried to blend in with the ninjas, Roman soldiers, faerie princesses, military people, medieval whatevers, and even a weird cartoon-type character on her way to the market.

Etain slipped past a small girl at the door and mingled with other customers, doing her best to imitate their actions of squeezing, smelling, and knocking on various fruits and vegetables. Everyone smiled and muttered general niceties to one another. Much to her delight, the owner set out samples for their enjoyment. She didn't care much for the melon but made sure to grab a couple of strawberries or grapes each time she passed the sample plates.

When she noticed the guy behind the counter watching her, she smiled and worked her way to the door. A quick look down the street showed no signs of the pesky boys. *Hallelujah.* The plan now was to visit the bakery in the other direction for a few carbs.

Etain stopped at the small girl standing alone amidst the jumble of grown-ups. Although she wasn't crying, she wasn't happy either, her little eyes following everyone who passed by. *Maybe she's lost?*

"Hi. Would you like a strawberry?" She crouched and held one in the palm of her hand. "It's really good." The little girl hesitated, distrust in her eyes. "Go on. I've had enough. If I eat another one, I might burst." Etain laughed, hoping to set the girl at ease.

The urchin snapped the piece of fruit from her hand and shoved it into her mouth. Her eyes widened.

"See? I told you so." Etain looked around. "Are you here by yourself?"

Tears welled in the little girl's grey eyes, a few trickling down her cheeks. "I'm sorry," she whispered. "I didn't know you were nice."

"There! There she is!"

Hearing the familiar voice, Etain's heart sank but she smiled at the little girl and smoothed her tousled hair. "It's okay." Dread crept over her as she pivoted on her heels and stood to face him.

"What're you doing with my little sister?" The Einstein from the morning blustered, putting on an impressive act for his urchin friends behind him. "We've been searching for her all day. What were you planning to do with her?"

Etain placed her hands on her hips. "She's been standing right here. Are you blind?"

He nervously eyed those who passed by. "Is it why you ran away? So we wouldn't find out you'd taken her?"

She glared at the puffed-up boy who fidgeted in front of his cronies. Bullies with nothing better to do. "I ran because you chased me."

"Yeah, well, you took my sister."

The other boys joined in with murmurs of support for their friend.

Etain checked behind her, but the girl was gone. "Looks like little sis has run off again. Maybe she doesn't like you or your...friends. Who you gonna chase now?" She turned toward the boys and came nose to nose with the blond boy. "Get out of my face."

"Oh, yeah?" He clearly struggled to hold her gaze. "What'd you do with my sister?"

"Seriously?" Etain stood her ground. "You just saw her standing right there!"

"You brainwashed her, didn't ya? Told her to hide until you got rid of us."

She glared at his friends, who shared the same dumb expression, and noticed other people watching their spat. *I'm out of here.* "How about you, your sister, and your girlies leave me alone." She stepped back and turned.

He grabbed her arm, but she shrugged him off. "Not until you give me my sister."

One of his cronies blocked her path. "You're not going anywhere."

Etain narrowed her eyes and smirked. "Why don't you be a good little boy and run after her?"

He bared his teeth and raised a fist. The blond boy grabbed her by the shoulders and twisted her to face him again. "You be a good little girl and do as I say."

Her knee jabbed into his groin. When he doubled over, she punched him in the jaw. The other boys formed a circle around her, punching and kicking. So frenzied in their attack, most of their hits missed their mark and landed on their friends, but she suffered enough. No one came to her defense. No one stepped in to stop the madness. She was a stranger in a strange place, and no one cared.

Etain fell to her knees amidst the insanity and vomited. Arms over her head, the violence brought to mind the murder of her parents, watching their bodies sliced into pieces in front of her. And her brother yelling. The terror of losing her family and chased by a red-eyed assassin, the smell of him around her, threatened to shred her defenses against a rising fear.

The silver orb shone in her mind's eye, its light a welcomed distraction from her current reality, and the man's voice—soft, deep, and comforting. She called him angel.

But it was clear there were no angels in the Alamir. Her fear fused with her disappointment and transformed into anger. In a surge of blue electrical charges, she rose to her feet, blasting everyone onto their backsides.

Her sights landed on the blond boy who initiated the fiasco. She stepped over the others until she stood over him. The blue charges still sparking around her, she grabbed him by the front of his shirt and pulled him up.

"If you want shit, Einstein, you got it."

He stared at her as though she'd lost her mind. "Put me down, you crazy bitch."

Her lips parted in a bloody smile and pointed a finger at him. "My name is Etain. Say it!" The blue sparks came close to his face, making him squirm. "Say it."

A tiny zap later, he squealed, "Etain!"

She set him down and eyed the others lying on the ground. None of them appeared to be injured by anything she'd done, except for Einstein, who totally deserved it. Not one of them met her gaze. "Little bitches. You messed with the wrong *girl*."

She forced herself to meet the silent judgment of those who watched, daring any one of them to come at her. *I'll zap you, too.*

Her anger cooled to a simmer. The blue charge sizzled with an occasional snap, crackle, and pop. *I'm a fucking rice crispy from hell.*

Without another word, she walked away.

WHEN THE POINTY END STICKS

E tain's heart thumped triple time, every cell in her body screaming at her to run and hide, punch something, cry. Yet, amidst the chaos, a sliver of steeled backbone placed one foot in front of the other and held her head high as she walked toward the edge of town. This was her first lesson as an Alamir—don't count on anyone. The only people who cared about her were dead.

But I have a weapon, she eyed the knife in the tongue of her boot, *and I have a power. I just need to learn how to use them.*

She kept to the cover of the lush countryside and followed the winding road as best she could. Should they come after her, she wanted the advantage of seeing them before they saw her. When a bridge presented itself, she left the road behind and followed the river. Although it would take longer to find the next town, the trees served as perfect targets to practice throwing the knife and gave her time to make sense of how quickly she was changing.

Time after time, she aimed and threw the knife. She tried at a distance. When it didn't work, she moved closer. Each time it bounced off the chosen target, but she refused to give up, even when the hunger pangs nagged at her.

I'll find something to eat once the pointy end sticks.

It finally sunk in that her release might be part of the problem. A memory of playing darts with her brother reminded her of what he called *follow-through*. If she held her wrist straight rather than flick it and followed through with her arm, her strike quota increased. Maybe it would work with the knife. Eventually, she saw some improvement. At least it hit what she aimed at. It just didn't stick.

The electrical charge was not as easily mastered. Neither was the knife, but it gave her something tangible to work with. Smart enough to know anger could be a great motivator, it wasn't how she wanted to live or activate her power. The incident at St Clears could have gone terribly wrong. But what other emotion would have the power to ignite the charge and control it?

Hunger pangs cut through the high of her small accomplishment with the knife.

Maybe I can stab a fish? She threw the knife again, hitting her intended mark. *But I'd have to eat it raw.*

She gagged at the thought and moved on, throwing the knife, and periodically trying to bring forth her electrical charge. *If I don't find food soon, I guess I'll have to try one of Dad's old tricks of eating tree bark. There's plenty of pines and birch around here.* Memories of those experiences turned her stomach. *Last resort only.*

The thoughts encouraged her out of the trees where she found a good-sized white cottage with thatched roof and flower boxes beneath the windows filled with an array of colorful blooms. Clothes on a line rippled in the gentle breeze, and beyond a big, red barn, cows grazed in a pasture. She'd seen pictures in story books, and of course, she'd watched every one of those fantasy movies with Hobbits and Elves. To see it in real life was awe inspiring. *Bilbo's sure to have something decent to eat.*

With the sun on its way down, it was time to take action on the hunger front or spend a miserable night with either an empty stomach or a bark dinner. She crept closer to the back of the cottage and peeked through an open window. On the cozy kitchen countertop sat a fresh handmade pizza. Her mouth watered. *God, it smells so good.* She scanned the room, but no one seemed to be around. *If you're gonna do it, do it now.*

She hurried to the rear door and carefully turned the knob. It wasn't locked. The pizza was too large for her alone, so she cut a couple of slices for herself, pieced the pizza back together as best she could, and wrapped her catch in a paper towel. Next to the pizza were bottles of soda.

The sound of laughter and footsteps in the hallway had her snatching a bottle and dashing out the door. As she made her way along the side of the house, she heard a woman call out, "Timothy Allen Ellis! Could you not wait for the rest of us?"

"What, Mum?"

"What have I told you about grabbing for yourself without a care?"

"Grabbing what?"

Etain bolted to the barn and stepped inside through the over-sized rolling door. A pair of snorting horses, one brown and the other white, surprised her. Her nose wrinkled at the smell.

Crap! Okay. Calm down. Take a deep breath. It's a barn. Of course, they'd have horses and there'd be farmy smells. If I'm nervous, they'll be nervous.

She relaxed against the wooden wall, breathed in, and gave the horses a lazy grin. "Hey, y'all."

Both animals shifted in their stalls, eyes on her. Slowly, she approached the brown one as she carried on with her one-sided conversation. "I promise I won't bother you." At the first stall, she set down her pizza and soda. "Hello, big guy, or girl. Sorry. I don't know which one you are. I hope you'll excuse the interruption and me being awkward. I've never met a horse much less talked to one, but I have some experience with dogs. Maybe it's kinda the same?"

She stood in front of the stall and let the horse come to her. After a sniff and snort, Etain lifted a steady hand and rubbed its nose.

"You're a beauty, aren't you? I hope this is okay. You're so grand."
The horse nudged at her. "I'll take it as a welcome."

She applied the same technique to the white horse and received
the same reception. "Thank you. I wish the people were as nice as
you two." As she rubbed its nose, she checked out the barn. At the
side of the main door was a ladder up to another floor. "Y'all don't
mind if I pop a squat up there, do you? I have a long day of walking
tomorrow. Don't ask me where I'm going 'cause I don't know. Silly
girl, huh?"

She bid her new friends a good night, climbed the ladder, and
snuggled into a corner amongst the hay where she savored every
bite of her prized pizza. *Sorry, Timothy*. Her belly full, she drifted
off to sleep.

⁓⣿⣶⣷⣶⣷⣶⡿⁓

Thanks to the Alamir farmer's early morning schedule, Etain was
up the moment the barn door opened. With a glance at the hint of
daylight through the gaps between the wooden slats of the walls,
she listened to him talking to his horses, doing whatever needed
doing before he set them free into the pasture, and pondered on
the prospect of snatching breakfast before continuing her sojourn
along the river.

You gotta be in and out. Fast and quick.

As soon as the three were out of the barn, she was down the
ladder and kept an eye on the farmer as she darted toward the
house. At the cottage, she peered through the back door window.
The kitchen was clear. After a check of the farmer's whereabouts,
she slipped inside.

Quick and fast. In and out.

A package of what resembled English muffins was on the countertop. She picked up the package. "What's a crumpet?" *It must*

be edible if it's in the kitchen. The moment she reached for the doorknob, someone came through an opposite door. Etain shoved the crumpets under her arm and opened the back door.

"Uh, hello."

She turned to a dark-haired boy, who couldn't have been much older than her. His heart had to be beating as fast as hers. "Hey."

A pink tinge touched his cheeks as he closed the door behind him. "Who are you?"

She noticed his accent. Not quite English but not American either. She shrugged and shifted on her feet. "Just someone passing through."

"You're pretty."

"What? Oh, uh, thanks." Her gaze darted to the floor and back to him. "You must be Timothy."

His dark eyes widened further. "How do you know my name?"

"I heard your mom yelling at you last night."

His brows furrowed before his eyes widened. "*You* took the pizza?"

She bit her bottom lip, giving him as sorrowful an expression as she could muster. "Sorry. I was super hungry."

"Hmph." Timothy shoved his hands into the back pockets of his jeans. "I had to eat beans on toast because of you. What're you doing here?"

"Like I said, just passing through."

His head tilted to one side. "Are you one of those independent Alamir?"

Familiar with the sound of snobbery, she frowned. "Not by choice. I'm trying to find a clan."

"You won't find one here."

She rolled her eyes. "I know. Are you in one?"

"Mum and Da are."

"Aren't you?"

A snort matched the tone of his voice. "Do I look old enough to be in one?"

"Well, if your parents are Alamir, aren't you?"

Timothy pulled his hands from his pockets. "Don't you know anything? You aren't *born* Alamir. You get initiated when it's your time."

Etain knew she had to get out before he made a grab for her or someone else walked into the room. "Oh. Yeah. I know."

"Who are you?"

"Well, thanks, Timothy. Maybe I'll see you around." She threw the package of crumpets at his head, pivoted on her heels, and ran like mad toward the treeline on the other side of the field away from where the cows grazed.

Partway, she glanced over her shoulder and saw the boy frantically pointing at her, but his sights were somewhere else, yelling at someone. *Aw, Timothy. You little shit.* Her gaze shifted to the farmer in the pasture, who had gotten a clue from his son's hysterics, and was heading her way.

Footsteps followed her deep into the forest, the farmer and his son yelling at her to stop. She ran until their voices faded and the footsteps disappeared. Another glance over her shoulder caused her to trip and sprawl out face first.

"Idiot. You're in a forest. Watch out for the huge roots." She sat up, spitting debris, and propped her arms on her knees. "Why the hell did you throw your breakfast at him?" With a roll of her eyes, she stood, swatting the dirt from her clothes, and caught a nasty whiff. "I need a wash."

She headed through the trees in the general direction of the river, and after a few adjustments, was soon rewarded by water gushing over rocks, bright sunshine sparkling like diamonds in the spray.

On the riverbank, she removed her boots, careful to hide the knife beneath them, and walked into the cool, crystal water, socks and all. She shivered but unbuttoned her top and unzipped her trousers for a quick handwash of the smelly bits and dunked her head. It wasn't the best way but better than nothing.

She took off her socks before walking onto the bank and laid them over the grass to dry while she searched for food. Wild blackberries were familiar, but she limited herself to only a few, enough to curb her immediate hunger. The last time she'd eaten the wild variety, they'd made her sick—when she was six and ate a sand bucket full of them. *Maybe my new Alamir belly is lined with cast iron.*

She laughed at her private joke but monitored her stomach for any signs of rebellion as she walked barefoot in the sunshine. "I wonder how far the next town is. Or maybe I should keep to myself." Standing at the river's edge, she stared across the water, hands on hips. "You'll never find a clan that way. No, I gotta go to however many towns it takes until a clan accepts me or... Or what?"

She lowered her head and closed her eyes. For several moments, she focused on the sounds around her. Birds twittering, water rushing, and the grass bowing to the songs of the trees as they danced in the wind. So peaceful. Her eyes opened as she lifted her head. "I'll figure it out."

TO BE ALAMIR

L ater in the day, she came to a town named Llansteffan, which was pretty much a twin to St. Clears, and walked straight into the town center. Her first order of business was to find the town hall and check for announcements of gatherings but found no joy on the notice boards.

The local market proved more fruitful. She made sure to steer clear of groups and scored a few nibbles. If anyone looked at her for too long, she immediately left the area. One thing her father *had* mentioned in his stories about the Alamir was news travelled fast. Gossip—the hot commodity of civilization.

A couple of hours later, she walked into Llangain. *All these towns with names I have no idea how to pronounce.*

On her way toward the center, she passed a small clothing store with a sign saying they bought used clothes in good shape. Etain checked her leathers. *I wonder what these are worth.*

An older woman greeted her as she stepped inside, the bell on the door tinkling. "*Prynhawn da*, please come in."

"Hi." Etain's gaze roamed over the tall salesclerk and the items in the shop. Along with used clothing, it held old books, dishes, glasses, shoes, even furniture.

"Are you looking for anything in particular?"

The woman sounded American and didn't seem threatening. Etain walked to the counter. "How much would you give me for these leathers? I just had them cleaned."

The brown-haired lady leaned over the counter for a quick inspection and eyed her from over the rim of her glasses. "Do you have another set of clothes?"

Etain ran a hand through her hair. "No. Why?"

The salesclerk leaned back, tapping her lips with a finger as she considered the offer. "What if we do a trade? Your leathers for another outfit."

She glanced out the front shop window thinking what a stupid idea it had been. "I don't have anything to trade for food. I need money."

"I see." The woman crossed her arms. "What if we do this? I'll give you a hundred pounds for your leathers and a few other items in trade."

Etain furrowed her brows. "A hundred pounds of what?"

The lady smiled. "It's money in this part of the realm."

"Oh."

"Your leathers are worth a lot more, but you'll have a better chance of getting them back." She walked around the counter to get a full view. "The boots?"

"You'd have to kill me first."

The woman chuckled. "Are you new to the Alamir?" At Etain's glare, she said, "I'm not mocking you. Be careful of your words in this world. Someone might accept them as a challenge." She pointed around the shop. "Choose a new outfit and a decent coat. You'll thank me come autumn. Get a brush for that mane, and a backpack. By the way, I'm Vivian."

"Why would you help me?"

Vivian turned to her. "It's what I would hope for if I were new. By the looks of you, I'd say it's not been easy."

Etain only shrugged.

"It's almost five. Have a browse around the shop while I lock up. I hope you'll join me for supper. I live upstairs."

"What's in it for you?" Etain already had her eye on a pair of black jeans. *There has to be a decent T-shirt in here somewhere.*

Vivian raised a brow. "A new friend, I hope."

She wasn't sold on the woman's story, but a free meal sounded good. "I'm Etain. Nice to meet you."

Their deal made and while Vivian completed her closing duties, Etain climbed the stairs to the second floor over the shop and stepped into a place of unexpected comfort. The room stretched from the front of the building to the back, a modern kitchen to her right, dining table in the center, and bohemian-style living room to her left.

Vivian, maybe you are worth getting to know.

She roamed about, touching trinkets from faraway places, admiring this and that. A doorway on the other side of the room led her into a hallway and the rest of the apartment, bedroom, bathroom, and office on the backside, and to the front, a large bedroom with its own bathroom.

"Selling old clothes must be big business in the Alamir." She caught her reflection in the mirror of Vivian's dressing table, "Holy shit," and leaned in for a closer look. "It's a wonder she didn't kick you out and lock the door." Etain pulled a twig from her hair and straightened.

At the bathroom, she glanced into the bedroom. Something her brother said to her time and again, "If it seems too good to be true..." He'd lean into her face. "It is."

Her backpack dropped to the floor. "I need a plan." She walked to the window in the bedroom and parted the curtains. It looked out onto a narrow, metal walkway that ran toward the room on the other side of the bath. She dashed to the office and checked its matching window. "Yes!" The walkway ended at a set of stairs.

Conscious of the time, she returned to the bath, turned on the water, and stripped, folding her leathers into a neat pile to give to Vivian later. The shower not only washed away the dirt and grime, it gave her a new perspective on future prospects.

Was Vivian in a clan she could join? Would they take a chance on someone with no experience?

I don't see why not. If you don't know you're destined to be Alamir, how can you be prepared?

Out of the shower, she swiped her hand across the mirror. "So what if you can't control the electric thing or do much with the knife other than throw it at stuff? You're growing and learning and meeting new people."

Her mother's words ran through her mind. *Faith is what it takes, my love. You can accomplish anything if you believe in yourself.*

She glared at herself in the mirror. "You *have* to move forward."

With a towel wrapped around her and one on her head, she carried her new backpack filled with the things she'd traded for into the bedroom. Another check of the window reassured her of an easy escape if needed. Then she sat on the comfy bed.

With Etain upstairs, Vivian seized the opportunity to reach out to a colleague using the new coms system they'd recently put in place. She adjusted the earpiece to a comfortable position.

"Sid, she's here."

"Are you sure?"

"Yes! The very one you were telling me about. Wild, silver hair, leathers, attitude." She chuckled. "You didn't tell me she was a kid."

"I didn't get close enough to tell. Things went down pretty quick in St. Clears. Me and Angel tried following her, but she was too quick for the likes of us. She obviously went cross country. Did you get a reading off her?"

Vivian listened to the sound of running water for a moment. Satisfied her guest was occupied, she said, "She's not like the others. I haven't been able to get through whatever's blocking me."

"Hmm. Do you think she's read you instead?"

"Gosh, I hadn't considered it." Vivian sighed. "If she had, she wouldn't have stayed. I've invited her to supper."

"Good. Me and Angel will come tonight."

Vivian pulled the cash drawer from the register. "No! You stay where you are. We have the advantage right now. Let's not squander it."

"How do you plan to keep it? You gonna tie her up and keep her in a closet?"

"I'm going to steer her to a gathering in Carmarthen. It's in a couple of days. If I'm lucky, I can get her to stay here with me to give you time to notify G and get over there." Vivian sensed his frustration. "Sid, she must make the choice."

"You seem pretty sure of yourself."

"Not me. Her. You'll see." Vivian nodded, certain she was right. "How's Angel?"

"Anxious to get home. It was supposed to be a quick trip."

"I know it's tough being on the road, but this girl is worth it. We can't afford to lose her." Vivian walked to the office, cash drawer in hand, and locked it in the safe.

"Do you think she could turn?"

"I don't believe she understands her power." She glanced over the office, turned off the light, and headed to the door at the back of the shop. "And I doubt the *Bok* have noticed yet. Let's see what I can find out tonight and get back to you. Send my love to Angel."

"You watch yourself, Viv. Don't go losing your wits over this girl."

She laughed. "I'll be fine. Talk to you soon."

Etain woke to full-on daylight and popped up, both towels still in place. "Man, I must've slept like the dead." She listened for any sound from Vivian as she unwrapped the towel from her head, but the apartment was quiet. The tinkle of the bell from the shop door downstairs made her stop. "What time *is* it?"

She wandered across the hall to Vivian's room and checked the office. No sign of the woman. The kitchen clock told her she'd slept well past noon. "Damn."

A note by the coffeemaker invited her to fix herself a cup and whatever else she'd like for breakfast, except the word *breakfast* was scratched out and replaced with *dinner*. "Ha. Funny lady. I'll skip the disgusting coffee but accept your offer of the food."

She returned to the bedroom, dressed, and straightened the room. In the kitchen, she whipped up scrambled eggs and toast but bypassed the coffee for juice. The dishes washed and set to dry, she grabbed her things and headed downstairs.

Vivian was busy with a customer at the counter, but smiled seeing her at the door. "Etain! You're up. Did you get a bite to eat?"

Etain gave her a timid smile and nodded as she walked to the counter. "Sorry I slept so long." She smiled at the customer. "Morning."

The old woman returned the smile. "*Prynhawn da*."

Unsure of what the woman said, Etain turned to Vivian. "You must've needed it. I'm glad you got some rest."

"Me too. I feel a lot better. Thank you. For everything. You've been way too kind."

Vivan handed the older woman her bag. "*Diolch*, Mrs. Bevan. *Prynhawn da*."

Once she was out the door, Etain asked, "Did some Alamir bring their grandmother here?"

"Mrs. Bevan is Alamir. She could be someone's grandmother. I don't know her that well."

"But she's so old."

Vivian laughed. "She wasn't old when she transitioned, Etain. Mrs. Bevan has been Alamir for a long time. In her younger days, she was known as Lady Death."

Her eyes widened. "Seriously? What does she do now? How could she fight off a demon?"

"Don't let her appearance fool you." Vivian winked. "It's true, she's not as physical as she used to be but she's a great instructor in the art of mind manipulation and still throws a mean punch."

Etain couldn't stop the laugh bubbling out of her. She covered her mouth and tried to appear appropriately regretful. "I'm sorry, Vivian. My dad told me a lot of stories about the Alamir but never said anything about anyone being old."

The woman raised a brow. "You'd do well to remember not to underestimate your opponent, young lady."

Her reprimand had no effect on Etain's grin. "I'll do my best. What was it she said to me? *Prawn da?*"

"*Prynhawn da* means good afternoon. It's Welsh."

"Okay." Etain glanced around the shop. "Well, I guess I'll—"

"It's dinnertime. Join me for a bite at the pub?" Vivian walked to the shop door and flipped the Open sign to Closed and turned the lock. "I'm starving."

She furrowed her brows. "What's a pub?"

Vivian turned with a curious smile on her face. "You've never been to a pub?"

Etain shoved her hands into her back pockets. "I've never heard of it."

"Oh, I'm sorry. You're not from around here, are you?" Vivian walked toward the back door. "Basically, it's a restaurant with a bar. In the olden days, they were called public houses."

Etain nodded thoughtfully. "Hence 'pub'."

Vivian grinned. "Such a clever girl. I'd like to get to know you better and I'm sure you have questions you'd like to ask. Grab your pack and let's chat."

At the counter, Etain grabbed her backpack, murmuring to herself, "Well, yes, Vivian, I do have a few questions. But can I trust your answers?" She shrugged the pack onto her shoulder and followed the woman outside.

Vivian walked to the end of the block and turned left at the corner. "The food's not as good as the company, but I think you'll enjoy the experience."

Midway down the road, Vivian stopped in front of a building straight out of a Shakesperean play, opened a large wooden door, and stepped through a tiny foyer into a large room filled wall to wall with people. Some sat at tables, some stood at the bar, and others were playing either darts or pool.

The smells of food and beer brought up memories of her parents. Dad usually enjoyed a cold brew at the end of a hard day and actually let her taste it once at his own peril. Mom was a bartender yet adamant alcohol would not pass her daughter's lips until she was at least fifty years old.

Although she smiled at the memory, upon spying the women's toilet, she veered that way and slipped into a stall. The front of her shirt gripped in both hands, she gasped for air and sank to her knees, unable to stop the tears or push away the pain. Her heart ached to the point she thought she would pass out. *I'm so sorry. I'm sorry. I hate this. I don't wanna be here. I don't wanna do this.* She covered her face with her hands. *I wanna be with you.*

Whether Etain was too engulfed in her pain, or the woman was a Class A ninja, Vivian appeared in the stall and kneeled in front of her, embracing her as though a mother consoling her child. If she had an opinion, she kept it to herself and held Etain while she cried.

Etain sniffled and lifted her head. No longer in the pub toilet, she recognized Vivian's apartment. "How'd we get here?"

Vivian gave her another hug and chuckled. "I'm not sure of the how. But I know who."

She rolled her eyes. "Another *gift*? I hope you're okay."

Vivian let go of her and pushed up from the floor, grabbing a towel from the kitchen counter. "A bit flustered but I'm good. It's an interesting way to travel."

She accepted the towel, wiping her eyes and nose, and leaned against the sofa. "Isn't it? I didn't know I could do that. I just wanted to go home but obviously it's not gonna happen."

"You didn't like the pub?" Vivian sat on the floor in front of her.

"What I saw was nice." She blew her nose into the towel. "Why are you being so nice to me? And please don't say it's so we can be friends. Everyone I've met so far has pretty much been pro ego."

Vivian frowned. "I had a difficult time when I first transitioned. Mine took me completely by surprise. At least you were told stories about the Alamir. I'd never heard of them until I found myself in the midst of what I now know was a clan bash."

Etain widened her eyes. "A clan bash?"

"It's when two clans..." Vivian met her gaze. "You know what a clan is, right?"

She hiccupped. "Oops. Sorry. Sometimes I get them when I cry or eat spicy stuff. Yes. I know about the clans."

"Good. Well, when two or more clans don't agree on territories or members, or about anything, really, they bash it out."

"What do they bash?"

"Each other."

Etain swiped at her runny nose. "You mean in the Mobius Arena?"

The woman seemed impressed. "A clan bash isn't as civilized. They've become brutal and have cut our numbers significantly."

"Alamir are killing Alamir?"

"Our new Ambassadors have been trying to get control of it." She pushed up from the floor and sat in the easy chair. "It's why they introduced the Mobius—to keep personal fights from escalating to full on bashes. But not everyone wants to change."

Etain leaned her head against the soft cushion of the sofa. "How stupid. Why fight each other when there's so many *other* things to fight, like demons and *Bok*?"

Vivian sighed. "Alamir are as diverse as humans but amplified. They bring their hate and prejudices with them, and some make no attempt to understand or accept those different from themselves. I don't know how the Ambassadors are going to solve the problem."

"But you found a clan, right? A good one?"

"They found me." Vivian propped her elbow on the arm of the chair and rested her head against her hand. "Luckily, they were there the day I transitioned and scooped me out of the mess before I lost my head. Literally."

Etain stretched her legs out in front of her. "Wish they'd been in the alley when I did."

"If you don't mind me asking, how did it happen for you?"

She placed her hands in her lap and lowered her eyes. Telling this stranger about the death of her family wasn't going to happen. It was too personal, too fresh. For all she knew, Vivian was a part of the conspiracy that killed them.

"Etain?"

"A silver orb," she blurted. Her gaze met the concern in the older woman's eyes. "A silver orb appeared and changed me. When I stepped out of the alley, I was here. In the Welsh sector."

Vivian leaned forward. She didn't need to read the girl's thoughts to know it had been a traumatic experience. The sadness on her face spoke volumes.

"I'm sorry, Etain," she said softly. "And you've not been treated well since coming here."

Etain lowered her eyes and shrugged. "I went to a gathering my first night. In St. Clears. I thought I was lucky. I was going to find a clan, make friends, and learn about being Alamir." Her blue-eyed gaze pierced through Vivian. "I told them I was new, and fourteen. But they didn't care. All they wanted was power and experience. How am I gonna get any experience if no one helps me?"

She eyed the girl for a long moment. "I don't condone what they did, but you don't look fourteen."

Etain came straight up off the floor. "I *am* fourteen! Or I was when the orb changed me." Vivian swore she saw a flash of violet in her eyes. "But now, all I know is I have boobs and a knife." She reached into her boot and brought out a pitiful excuse for a weapon, slamming it on the table. "And I can do this." The girl closed her eyes and within moments a blue glow sparking with electrical currents surrounded her. When she opened her eyes, they glowed ice blue.

Vivian stared at her, speechless. Before she could retain her senses, Etain grabbed the knife and her pack, dashed to the door, and was gone.

The sound of a slamming door snapped Vivian from her shocked stupor. She raced out of the flat and down the stairs to the door that served as her private entrance from the street. Or had served. The lever handle lay broken on the outside walk and the door hung on warped hinges. It had been locked from the inside and the keys were in her pocket. In a daze, she searched up and down the road, but there was no sign of the girl.

What in the hell are we going to do with you?

NEVER FORGOTTEN

V ivian went inside to the shop, checked the lock on the front door, stashed the cash drawer in the safe, turned off the lights, and locked the back door on her way out. Upstairs, she changed out of her dress and sensible shoes into jeans, a flannel shirt, and boots. Her hair pulled back into a ponytail, she sped down the stairs.

Around the corner and a couple of doors down the road, she checked in with a good friend who happened to be a locksmith.

"Afternoon, Len."

He lifted his head, smiled, and turned off the grinder. "Afternoon, Viv. What brings you round this time of day? Extended break?"

"Not exactly." She laid the handle on his bench.

Len eyed the piece. "What happened?"

"I don't have time to explain." She shifted on her feet. "Can you fix it?"

"What am I fixing?"

"The handle, lock..." She sighed. "Well, the whole damn door."

He cocked a brow. "It's not my—"

"Do what you can. I have to go."

As she stepped out the door, he called out, "Come by later and pick up the keys."

With a satisfied smile, she followed the trail of electrical residue left behind by her new Alamir friend.

Etain ran until the blue sparks faded; her breath failing at the same time. She stumbled off the pavement onto the grassy shoulder and ended up rolling down a slight incline into an adjoining field. On her side, she shucked off the backpack, sucking in air.

Control. You gotta learn control.

Able to breathe easier, she sat up and ran a hand through her hair. "What the fuck, Etain? You can't run away from everything."

"You all right down there?"

Great. From over her shoulder, she looked at Vivian standing at the roadside. It surprised her in two ways. First, the woman came after her, and two, seeing her made her want to cry, which she did.

Vivan frowned, walking down the incline, and crouched in front of her.

"I'm sorry, Vivian." Etain raised her tear-stained face. "I'm such an idiot."

"Don't be so hard on yourself. You've experienced the biggest fubar of your life, Etain. It'll take time to adjust."

"I feel like such a baby."

"Well, you are. Don't be offended. Everyone is when they first transition. They have no idea what it means to be Alamir. But in your case, you truly *are* a baby. Fourteen is too young."

Etain blinked several times. "You believe me?"

Vivian reached out and gently squeezed her upper arm. "Yes, I do."

"Why you and no one else?"

With a tilt of her head, she rubbed Etain's arm hoping the connection would give her some comfort. "What purpose would it serve to lie about your age?"

Etain shrugged and sniffled. "I don't know. I've seen others younger than me."

Vivian sat back. "It's my guess their parents turned before they were born."

Her eyes widened. "People have babies here?"

The woman chuckled. "We're still human. Humans with extra-ordinary powers, but the basics remain the same. People meet, fall in love, have families. Argue."

"Yeah. I've met a few. Kids, I mean." She stared across the field. "Guess they thought I was one of them."

"Did you make friends?"

"We played a few games," Etain met her gaze, "but I beat them. They didn't seem too happy about it, so I left."

Vivian stood and held out a hand. "Let me teach you things your father's stories did not."

She squinted at the woman giving no indication she would accept. "If you play games with me, I'll beat you, too."

Vivian's hand remained extended, but the smile disappeared. "I'm not much of a gamer. Come on, take my hand."

"Are you in a clan?"

"Not really."

Etain ignored the offered hand and came to her feet. "Either you are, or you aren't. What happened to the one that saved you?"

Vivian sighed and dropped the offer. "Clans come and go. I moved on."

Etain slung her backpack over her shoulder. "Whatever you think you're offering, no thanks. I'll figure it out on my own."

"I haven't been in a clan for a long time, but I have connections."

"More of the bullshit." Etain turned to go. "Bye, Vivian."

"Wait." She grabbed her by the arm. "There's another gathering in a couple of days in a town not far from here. Stay with me until then. I swear you won't regret it." She raised a hopeful brow. "Help out in the shop and meet a few real Alamir."

She considered her options, doing a quick pros vs cons list in her head, food and shelter being at the top of the pros. "Two days, that's it. No trying to make me stay longer."

"With the power you showed me?" Vivian shook her head. "I'd be crazy to try. Look, at some point, you're going to have to trust someone. Let me prove I'm the one."

Etain walked with her to the road. "What's your power, Vivian?"

"I hear peoples' thoughts and sometimes *persuade* them to do what I tell them to do. But they think it's their idea."

"Hmph. Are you hearing my thoughts?" She raised a brow. "Are you the reason why I'm walking into town instead of out?"

Vivian grinned. "One doesn't need to *listen* to your thoughts. Your face pretty much tells the story."

Etain frowned. "My face?"

"You're rather expressive."

She bit the inside of her bottom lip. "Yeah, it needs work too." They walked a few more steps before she asked, "You swear you're not manipulating my thoughts?"

"I am not, nor am I able to. You're the first person I've met who I can't read, so your thoughts are safe in that head of yours."

"Cool." Etain glanced at her from the side of her eye. "You aren't lying to me, are you?"

Vivian stopped. "What does your gut tell you?"

She also stopped and thoughtfully considered the question. "My gut says you're definitely crazy," she chuckled, "but good people. Most would run from someone like me, especially after the show I put on."

Vivian laughed as they resumed their walk to the shop. "A little crazy never hurt anyone."

"I guess so," Etain said, certain she was perhaps more than a little. "One thing I've been wondering."

"What's that?"

"How do you pronounce the name of the town? I understand it's Welsh, but how the heck do the two L's work?"

"It depends on who you ask. I've been trying to perfect it myself." She stopped again. "Bear with me. It takes some concentration on my part. The easiest way to get close to making the proper sound is to press your tongue against the ridge just behind your upper teeth." She opened her mouth to show Etain. "Like this."

Etain felt the ridge with the end of her tongue.

"Now blow air from your cheeks, not your throat, your cheeks. Llangain."

Etain made several attempts, each one ending in laughter. "I'm not much of a linguist."

Vivian laughed with her. "Even if you pronounce it as an 'L', the locals will know what you mean. They might give you a cheeky smile, but they'll understand."

"I think I'll ask where the next town is instead of saying the name."

"I can teach you a few sayings. If you're going to be in the Welsh district, you should learn as much as you can."

"Well, my ultimate plan is to get back home to Texas, but I have things to do first. I figure, or hope, the orb sent me here for a reason."

"Any idea what it could be?"

She slipped her hands into her pockets. "I, uh..."

"Never mind. Tell me when you're ready, or don't." Vivian shrugged. "All that matters is I've been chosen by the same Lady Fate who brought you here to teach you what I can in the time we have."

"Thank you, Vivian." They resumed their walk back to town. "Where are you from originally?"

"I was born in California and transitioned when I was in my early twenties."

"How did it happen for you?"

"It ended in a bright glow but only after my head was ripped in two."

"What?" Etain tried to imagine her head split down the middle, wondering how she fixed it.

"Not literally. But it certainly felt like it."

"Like a migraine?" She'd never experienced one herself, but a friend had suffered from them and sometimes missed school for days.

"Worse. It lasted a couple of days before it took my sight. One night, as the pain subsided enough to fall asleep, a bright light flashed." She placed both hands on her head. "I thought my head had exploded. When the light faded, I was in the middle of a field, swords clanging and horses screaming."

"Could you see anything?"

She lowered her hands, shaking her head. "I saw plenty and wished I couldn't. I was so scared I vomited."

"I have a few times. Did you have a family? Friends? In the human realm."

Etain sensed the sudden sadness in the woman.

She wouldn't meet her gaze. "I did. No children," her voice faltered, "but I had a husband, who I loved more than life itself, and friends I would die for."

A pang hit Etain in her heart. "Did you try to go back?"

Vivian glanced at her and drew in a long breath. "Once. Long enough to know I had changed too much for it to work."

"How did your husband take it?"

"Oh, well, I never approached him. It was best he thought I'd been a kidnap/murder victim than know I was alive in a world where he couldn't go."

Etain shook her head and pursed her lips. "I'd much rather know someone I loved was alive and well than rotting in the ground, or worse, had left me without a word."

They stepped onto the lane leading to the shop. "Are you sure you're only fourteen?"

Etain raised a brow and tilted her head with a shrug. "Not anymore. I remember things I did not long ago in my old life. They seem so ridiculous. There's other things I try not to think about because it hurts too much."

"Insightful. I hope one day you'll trust me enough to share your story." At the door to her apartment, she said, "Stay here for a sec. I need to pop around the corner for the key."

Etain leaned against the brick wall and watched Vivian disappear down the street. *What's a couple of days? Maybe she can give me some tips on how to get a clan to accept me. It's worth your time. Be patient.*

Vivian soon returned with the key in hand. "My friend, Lenny, he's a locksmith, repaired the handle and lock for me. But with a closer look, I think I have a new door, too."

"Oh. I broke it, didn't I? I'm sorry, Viv—"

"Don't fret over it. Shit happens, right?" She opened the door and let Etain in first. "Why don't we both get a wash. Afterwards, we can have a long chat and maybe I can fix us a nice supper."

"You don't have another set of jeans and T-shirt, do you? These are kinda muddy from the field."

"I can lend you one of my dresses for tonight." Vivian grinned. "You don't mind wearing one, do you?"

"As long as I can trade it for jeans tomorrow."

The next morning, Etain woke to a fresh pair of jeans and a black AC/DC T-shirt at the foot of her bed. "Maybe she *can* read my mind." She smiled at herself in the mirror as she brushed out her hair. "What if I stayed here?" She set the brush on the bathroom countertop. "Is it absolutely necessary to run off to another town where you don't know anyone? Take another chance like the last one? Vivian likes me. I like her. It could work."

Etain turned to leave the room when another voice penetrated her thoughts.

"*What about us?*"

She froze, her heart pounding. "What?"

"*Your family. Are we so easily forgotten? It's your job to avenge our deaths.*"

"Dad?" She turned as if he might appear in front of her.

"*The first nice person you meet and you're ready to trade us off for a cozy life?*"

"No! It's not like that." Etain ran both hands through her hair. "I don't know what I'm doing. I need to learn how to fight, how to use a sword. Vivian's going to teach me, then I can go after the demon."

"*Remember where you come from. Never give up.*"

"Dad? Dad! Please come back." She sat on the bed, fighting the urge to cry. *Was it him, or my guilty conscience?* She shook her head. *Two days, Etain. Two days and you're gone.*

Vivian's heart lifted when the girl came into the kitchen dressed in the jeans and T-shirt she'd left in her room. *I chose well.* But she sensed darkness in her mood. *Don't push. You have to let her come to you.*

"*Bore da*, Etain. That's 'good morning' in Welsh. How'd you sleep?"

The girl rambled around the room lost in thought. "*Bore da*, Vivian. Okay, I guess."

"You seem distracted."

"Huh? Oh. Maybe."

Vivian watched her roam from the sofa to the dining table, her gaze drifting toward the door now and then. "Are you expecting someone?"

Etain furrowed her brows. "What? No."

"Why don't you set the table? You know where the plates and silverware are, right?"

"Yeah, okay." She pulled two plates from the open shelf next to Vivian's head and went around to the drawer beside her and grabbed a couple of forks and knives. As she set the table, she asked, "How soon can we get to the Alamir stuff?"

"How about we eat breakfast first, then we can decide how the day's going to go."

"Well, we only have two days. I don't want to waste any time."

Vivian bit her tongue and swallowed a sharp retort, stirring the scrambled eggs as she faced Etain. "About that." The blue-eyed glare she received made her breath catch. *Go easy, Vivian.* "I received word this morning that the gathering has been postponed a few days."

She shifted on her feet, resting a hand on her hip. "Convenient, don't you think?"

Keep your cool. Do not let this little upstart rattle you. She forced herself to act nonchalant and returned to the eggs. "Not at all. The *Bok* have been spotted near the town where it's to take place. With new recruits headed there, the Ambassadors have ordered the larger clans to sweep the area and make sure it's safe."

Etain slouched in her chair, an arrogant smirk on her face. "And I guess you're expecting me to stick around?"

Vivian turned off the burner and carried the skillet to the table where she slammed it down. A portion of the eggs bounced out of the skillet. "I don't know what's crawled up your ass today, but I will not tolerate you acting like a sarcastic shithead."

The girl straightened in her chair, eyes wide.

"It is *not* convenient, and sister, you have nothing *but* time. You choose how you want to spend it. Be the brat you're proving yourself to be or show some gratitude to a few good people who have decided you're worth their time and effort. You may not get another chance like this one, Etain."

Afraid she might throw the skillet at the girl, Vivian stormed to the door and slammed it behind her before stomping down the stairs. Once outside, she blew out a heated breath, her hands on her hips, pacing back and forth. "Saints help me. Why am I bothering?"

The town's blacksmith, a brown headed bull of a man with a full beard and wearing his smithy apron, came from around the corner. "Miss Vivian, *bore da*. You all right?"

"I'm fine, Jacob." She continued pacing in front of the door.

He grinned. "Are you sure? I can't say as I've ever seen you like this."

She stopped and faced him. "It's that *girl* upstairs. The one who came into the shop the other day."

He raised a brow. "The one you were telling us about at the pub? You got her to stay?"

"To my own detriment. I thought she would appreciate what we're trying to do for her, but no, she's an ungrateful little brat who has no manners whatsoever. She's no different from the others."

He stroked his beard in thought. "Hmm. Didn't you say she's a young one? Need I remind you of their temperamental ways?"

She sighed and laughed at herself. "Oh, Jacob. You're right, of course. Did I tell you she's only fourteen?"

His brows rose. "No, but—"

"There are moments when I forget how young she is and believe in the façade. She's so intelligent, and at times, mature beyond her years. But *this* morning, I would love to throttle the little monster."

At that moment, the door opened. Vivian moved to the edge of the walk as the girl stepped outside.

Etain quietly closed the door, looking every bit the contrite fourteen-year-old.

"Vivian..." she started, then noticed the big man a few steps away. "Uh, I-I'm sorry to interrupt." She reached for the door handle.

"Etain..." Vivian said fervently. She closed her eyes, took a breath, and tried again. "Etain, meet Jacob. He's the town's blacksmith and a good friend."

She released the handle and held out her hand. "Nice to meet you, Jacob. I'm Etain."

His large hand engulfed her smaller, delicate one, but she gave as good as she got. "Nice to meet you, Etain. That's some grip you have there."

A worried frown on her face, she let go of his hand. "I didn't hurt you, did I?"

Jacob's jolly laugh took her by surprise and made her blush. "Did you hear that, Viv? Worried that *she* hurt *me*." He swiped at the tears in the corners of his eyes. "What a good one."

Vivian smiled; her anger forgotten. "Well, she *is* the reason why Len had to replace my door."

His brows rose. "This one?"

Vivian nodded and winked at Etain, who appeared more lost than ever. "Jacob, have you come by for a reason?"

"Oh, aye!" From his back, he brought forth a sword, feminine in style. "It didn't take as long as usual, it being small."

"I wasn't expecting it so soon." Vivian took the blade from his hands. "It's lovely. Thank you." She turned to the girl. "Etain, it isn't fancy, but this is for you. I think it will fit nicely in your hand."

Etain crossed her arms and stared at the blade. "A sword? For me?" Her eyes reflected a sudden sadness as they met Jacob's. "But I don't know how to use one."

"We're going to teach you," Vivian said proudly.

The blue-eyed gaze turned to her. "You are?"

"Did you think I would send you into the Alamir world with only a butcher knife?"

"That reminds me." Jacob pulled what looked to a be an over-sized toothpick from his belt. But in Etain's hand, it transformed into a finely forged dagger. "Come by one day and I'll fashion a scabbard you can slip into your boot."

"Uh, thank you. You're too kind, both of you. I don't de-serve—"

"Nonsense," Vivian said. "Moments like these don't come often in an Alamir life, so you grab them and hold on for as long as you can."

"Aye. Truer words were never spoken. I have to get back to my forge. *Ta-ta tan toc.*" Jacob waved as he turned.

"Thanks again, Jacob," Vivian called out.

"Vivian." Etain touched her on the arm. "I'm sorry for earli-er and acting like a douche. I *do* appreciate what you're doing. Not that it's an excuse, but memories of my family came out of nowhere and, well—"

"Enough said. We still have breakfast to do, don't we? I can't teach you how to fight on an empty stomach."

TOY SWORDS

In a yard behind the smithy's shop, Vivian and Etain faced one another, wooden sword to wooden sword.

"Why are we using toys?"

"Because the Alamir bleed and if you lose a body part, it doesn't grow back." Vivian raised a brow. "Unless you prefer—"

"No, no, I get it." Etain licked her lips. "Baby steps."

"Exactly. Before we get to the swords, let's work on our stance." Vivian placed hers on the ground.

Etain screwed up her face. "What are you doing?"

"You have to have a stable base, balance. Put your sword down."

Etain dropped her sword and raised her hands in a boxer's stance. "Is this what you're talking about?"

Vivian rested her hands on her hips, checking the girl's form. "Not bad."

"My brother taught me a few things. Not about swords," she lifted her shoulder in a half-shrug, "but some boxing moves."

Vivian sensed a tragedy involving her family had brought the girl to the Alamir but respected her privacy and had not pushed for more information. At the same time, she believed she needed to share her story with someone and get it out of her head. Maybe the focus on other things would help her let go of their ghosts and move on. Whether she liked it or not, this was her life.

"A boxer?" Vivian circled around her.

"Nah. He loved wrestling but had friends who boxed. They taught him and he taught me."

"Good form and foot placement, knees bent. Shoulders and arms relaxed. Elbows down and in, hands up, chin down. Fists not too tight." She stopped in front of her. "It *looks* good but can you—"

Etain caught her by surprise when she snapped out with a right jab and knocked her onto her backside. "Yes, I can hit."

Jacob ran into the yard. "Viv!"

She rubbed her jaw with one hand as she waved the other. "I'm okay. Ask a silly question..." She noticed the girl was posed for another go if challenged. *Good.* Vivian came to her feet. "We have established you can hit."

Etain narrowed her eyes. "Are you gonna come at me?"

"Not at this moment." She picked up one of the wooden swords. "But no promises while we're sparring. Get your sword."

Etain glanced at Jacob and back at Vivian. With the wooden blade in hand, she set her feet in her boxing stance. "So this works with a sword, too?"

"It will serve you well with the one Jacob has made but keep your chin up." Vivian stood beside her. "You'll minimize your opponent's target yet maintain the ability to thrust. Don't be afraid to make adjustments as we get more into it. Do what feels right for you, but most importantly," she gave her a wink, "stay away from the pointy end."

Etain copied Vivian, holding her sword in front of her.

"Let's work on your grip."

Etain huffed. "How else would you hold it? This is the handle, right?"

"This part is the hilt." Vivian demonstrated with her own sword. She switched the weapon to her other hand and held her right hand out, palm up. "See these two mounds at the bottom of your hand?"

Etain eyed Vivian's hand and compared it to hers.

"And the valley between the two?" Vivian ran a finger along her palm. "The narrow side of the hilt should rest in the valley and your fingers should be at an angle just beyond the guard. It's this piece here." She held the sword in front of her to show how it fit perfectly between the two mounds and curled her first two fingers and thumb around it. She watched as Etain did the same. "Remember, it is a sword, not a hammer, so we hold it more with the first two fingers and the thumb."

"What about my other fingers?"

"Not too close to the guard. There you go. The other two fingers should be loosely curled around the hilt. It will give you more control."

They worked on Etain's grip until it felt comfortable. "I thought you grabbed and jabbed. I didn't realize how much finesse it takes."

"And a lot of practice." Vivian pointed at the rounded end of the sword. "This bit here is called the pommel. It acts as a counterweight. This longer piece in front of your hand is the guard, which is exactly what it's for, to guard."

She watched as Etain did a few practice moves.

"Let's try a few blocks. We'll go slow at first and build our speed. Remember, keep your chin up."

Later in the afternoon, they broke for a quick lunch and were back at it in less than a half hour. Etain soaked in every instruction excited to try new moves and proved to be as relentless as Vivian. She even sparred with Jacob for a short while. It mainly consisted of tapping blades but it gave her a taste of how it felt to face an opponent.

"Tomorrow we'll get your dagger in the mix," Jacob said as he walked the ladies to the door. "I'll show you how to use it with your sword."

Etain's eyes brightened. "I get to use my real sword tomorrow?"

Jacob's belly jiggled when he laughed. "*Bendithia fy enaid*, Viv (Bless my soul, Viv). I think we've opened a Pandora's box!"

Vivian's mouth curved into a wicked smile. "They'll never see her coming."

⁓⸻❦❦❦⸻⁓

The days turned into weeks. Jacob took over her training with the sword and dagger, his brutal style leaving her with cuts and bruises over most of her body. Just as she appeared to be competent with a move, he would change the game and throw her off kilter.

"You have to think fast and move faster. Be ahead of your opponent because if he or she thinks ahead of you, you're dead." He held out a hand to help her onto her feet. "Or in a very compromising position."

Etain brushed the dirt from her aching backside. "How am I supposed to learn all this in a few weeks?"

Jacob chuckled. "You won't, but I'm going to show you everything I know so when you get your arse kicked, and you will, you'll remember what we did here and won't let it happen again."

She picked up her sword and swept an arm across her sweaty brow. "Okay, if you don't knock it out of me before I have the chance to get it in there."

He down right laughed. "Hard knocks are going to keep you alive. No matter how many times you fall, get your arse up and keep fighting. Never give up. If you do, you're dead."

Etain took her stance again, sword in one hand and dagger in the other.

"Hard knocks are fine, Jacob," Vivian called out from the side lines, "but please leave enough sense in her for this afternoon."

"No promises, Viv," he said as he turned his claymore toward a nimble-footed Etain, who ducked and rolled across the ground out of harm's way.

"Are you looking to kill me, Jacob?"

He pivoted on a heel, swinging his sword round. "There's plenty out there bigger 'n me with a lot more power."

She skipped back a few steps. "Then I'll outrun 'em."

He cut back, just missing her mid-drift. "Nowhere to run in battle. You stand and fight or—"

"Yeah, you're dead."

He lifted his blade over his head and slashed down. In a panic, Etain fell to a knee but had the forethought to cross her blades above her head. At impact, her electrical charge surged forward through her blades into the claymore, sizzling into each of Jacob's hands and up his arms. The man and his sword flew backward across the yard into the stone wall of his shop and slumped to the ground.

"Jacob!" Both women yelled at the same time.

Etain threw down her weapons and was on her feet in an instant. She reached the unconscious man two steps after Vivian and dropped to her knees. "Holy crap! I'm so sorry! Jacob? Is he okay?"

"Jacob." Vivian felt his neck for a pulse. "His heart's good." She checked his eyes. "Jacob. Can you hear me? Jacob."

Etain grabbed his hand squeezing it between hers. "I'm such an idiot. I didn't mean to—"

"What were you thinking, Etain? It was a dirty move. Stay with him. I need to get some water." Vivian disappeared into the shop.

Etain touched his face. "Please be okay, Jacob. I didn't mean to hurt you. I was trying to—"

"Not get dead," he mumbled.

"Oh my god. Vivian! He's awake." She squeezed his hand again. "I'm so sorry. It came out of nowhere."

The woman appeared with a cloth thrown over her shoulder, a bowl under her arm, and a large bottle of water in her hand. "Move over, Etain."

"No. I'll do it."

Despite her annoyed expression, she handed the cloth to Etain, set the bowl down, and poured water into it. Etain dunked the cloth and wrung out the excess.

Jacob glared at Vivian. "Did you know?"

Etain dabbed at his face and forehead. "It's not her fault. She's only seen it the one time."

Her admission didn't do much to soften the fierceness in his eyes. "Doesn't matter. You could've mentioned it, Viv, before I let loose on the girl."

She crouched across from Etain every bit as fierce as him. "If I'd known you were going to go full on Attila, perhaps I would've. Serves you right."

"Give me a drink," he ordered as Etain rinsed the cloth and dabbed at his neck. After a long draw, he poured the rest over his head and sat up, forcing the women back. "We can't have you going off like that, Etain. Someone might end up dead, me being the someone." He turned to Vivian. "We've got to tell G."

Etain thought the woman looked almost apologetic.

"He knows," she whispered.

"What was that?" Jacob asked in a loud voice.

Vivian sighed and raised her voice. "He knows."

"Bloody hell!" Jacob pushed against the wall and onto his feet. "Where the hell is the man? We don't have what she needs." He stormed toward the back door of his shop. "Send in the sacrificial lamb. See what happens before his Highness shows his ugly face."

Vivian rolled her eyes as she stood and went after him. "Jacob!"

Etain sat cross-legged on the grass, listening to their conversation, contemplating her urge to run.

If anyone's the sacrificial lamb, it's me.

Who's this G person? Why didn't she tell me about him? She certainly told him about me.

She pulled at the grass, casting the blades to the wind.

Hmph. She didn't mention Jacob either. Maybe we aren't friends at all.

Things sounded pretty heated inside the shop. She stood, walked across the yard, and picked up her sword and dagger. "Should I stay on the chance these people have good intentions, or do I go?"

She tilted her head when Vivian appeared at the back door and abruptly stopped, a shocked expression on her face.

"Yeah. I'm still here. How's Jacob?" Etain returned to her crossed leg position.

The woman gave her a nervous smile as she cleared her throat in an obvious attempt to compose herself. Vivian stepped into the yard and walked toward her. "He's good, just taken by surprise."

Etain wanted to laugh at the absurdity of the situation but kept a straight face. "I'm sure it doesn't happen often."

Vivian joined her on the grass. "No, it doesn't, but hey," she touched Etain's hand and gave it a light squeeze, "it was *my* fault, not yours. I should've told him about your power."

Etain narrowed her eyes. "What's your game, Vivian? My whole life, I've been able to read people, even as a baby. But you make me doubt my abilities."

The woman let go of her hand. Her warm, empathetic expression hardened into one of a warrior. "Etain, I only want to help you."

"Who's this *G* guy you and Jacob were talking about? Is he some pimp you plan on selling me to?"

"You're completely off base." She leaned back and gazed at the sky for a moment. "In my former life, before coming to the Alamir, I was a teacher. A passion I still have, so I teach new Alamir about their world and how to protect themselves."

"Before you sell them off?"

"Stop it, Etain," she snapped. "I shouldn't have to constantly remind you to listen to your gut."

"I'm trying to but then you talk about me behind my back and what I thought was real turns to shit." She jumped to her feet. "Why am I the only one? You said there were others headed to this gathering. Why aren't you helping them?"

"Because I'm working with you."

"So you teach one at a time? How'd I get so lucky?"

Vivian shrugged a shoulder in a matter-of-fact way. "In some instances, when the student shows promise."

Etain closed her eyes and huffed. "What promise?"

Vivian stood and took hold of her shoulders. "The fact you're here at the age of fourteen tells me how special you are. If you'll give me the time, we can find out why."

Etain glared at her easy words. "*Is* there a gathering or was that bullshit?"

"I have no reason to lie to you." She let her go. "The gathering *was* delayed but why go? You can stay here with us, let us train you properly, and we can find out why you've transitioned at such an early age. Don't you want to know?"

Etain grabbed her dagger, slid it into her boot, and picked up her sword. "I have other things on my mind."

"If you insist on leaving," Vivian turned as Etain stepped past her, "there's a map in your pack. The way will take a little longer, but it keeps you off the main roads. And no fires. The *Bok* may still be around. And not all Alamir are honorable." When she reached the door, Vivian called out, "I can go with you."

Etain stopped and spoke over her shoulder. "No. I have to do this myself."

"Okay, well, you don't but it's your decision. Take the heavy cloak in the wardrobe in your room. Guaranteed it will rain at some point on your journey."

Her thoughtfulness cooled Etain's anger. "Thanks for everything, Vivian. Please thank Jacob and Len, too."

"I will. Please take care, Etain."

GREEN APPLES

L ate in the afternoon, the rain Vivian had forecasted made
its appearance. It was different from the rains in Texas that
brought relief from the scorching heat. This rain was cold, invasive,
and took the chill right down to the bone. Etain shivered as she
ducked under a group of large trees and draped the cloak over her
shoulders, fastening the silver clasp at her throat.

Protected from the elements, her attention turned to the hunger
pangs gnawing in her stomach. She found a few sandwiches in her
backpack wrapped in brown paper and chocolate-chip cookies in
a paper bag. She rolled her eyes and chuckled.

"Thanks, Vivian. Now I feel like a complete asshole."

The further she'd gotten from the town, the more she sec-
ond-guessed her decision to go. Granted, she had been tempted to
stay, have a warm place to sleep, and food to eat. On the other hand,
the need to search out her family's assassin, and kill him, gnawed
at her worse than her growling tummy.

She leaned against a tree as she grabbed one of the sandwiches
and carefully unwrapped one side, eating it slowly. Her first days
in the Alamir burned bright in her mind.

No telling when I'll get another meal after these are gone.

She watched the rain pelt the swaying green grasses and the
nearby river. The pat-pat-pat against the leaves overhead gave her
some comfort as she chewed her food.

I have skills. Vivian saw my potential. Surely, there are others who will train a novice.

Finished with half the sandwich, she wrapped the other side tightly in its brown paper and returned it to her pack. Rearranging the sandwiches, she saw the map and slipped it into her back pocket but happened to notice something else in her pack. "What? No." She pulled the sandwiches out, laying them on the ground, and returned to the pack. "Vivian." Folded and tucked in the bottom of her pack, she found her leathers.

"I'm such a dick." She left them there, afraid she'd never get them refolded so perfectly, and sighed at the gray day as she piled the sandwiches on top and secured the straps of the bag.

It has to be getting close to evening. Maybe another hour or two and I'll stop for the night.

A quick check of the map assured her she was on course and could follow the river within the safe confines of the forest. The hood of the cloak over her head, she faded into the shadows of the trees, careful to stay within eying distance of her river guide. As the day waned with only a sliver of light left in the sky, she called it a day.

Not in possession of a sleeping bag and nothing more than the leafy canopy above her as protection against the rain, she searched for some type of ground shelter for the night. Mostly what she found were smaller trees and massive tree trunks. When nothing presented itself, her sights turned upward.

Those trees tall enough to give her a place to rest had no branches low enough to make it easy to get a foot up. Not that it wasn't worth the effort to be safe but if she could find the one perfect tree with low lying branches it would make her life easier. She finally gave up the search and tried several running starts toward various possibilities but between the backpack, the cloak, and her boots, each attempt turned into instant failure. Thanks to the rain-soaked forest floor, the soles of her boots slipped on the bark, making it difficult to get any traction.

Her latest endeavor ended with a rough introduction of her face against the flesh of the tree. She yelped and fell on her back, electrical currents flashing each time her fists hit the ground. "Damn it. Damn it. Damn it."

Etain swiped at the salty tears stinging the scrapes on her cheeks and realized she wasn't alone. A small boy dressed in only a pair of shabby pants stood a few feet in front of her. He appeared to be alone but she remained wary and rolled to her feet, rubbing her hands together to remove the grit. "Where'd you come from?"

The boy didn't speak, nor did he move other than his eyes rolling upward to the darkening sky.

"Do you need help?"

His light eyes came back to her, shaking his head.

Etain shifted on her feet. "Look, I love a good eye roll. I've use them a time or two but I'm not getting whatever it is you're trying to say. So why don't you say it and I can get back to doing what I was doing, and you can move on."

He held out his hand and moved toward her. She stepped back into a boxing stance but kept her hands loose at her sides. The boy sighed and stared at her, his lips pressed together in bewilderment. In the next moment, he brightened and pointed two fingers at his eyes, at her, and back at himself. She shrugged. Again, he rolled his eyes.

When he walked straight at her, her body tensed, prepared to lash out, but he proved stronger than she expected, placed his hands on her arms, and made her turn around. He pointed straight ahead.

Not even six feet away stood a lovely, large tree with wide, luscious branches, perfect for climbing and a good night's sleep. *How did I miss it?*

"You were there?"

He stood at her side, pressed his hands together and rested his head on them, closing his eyes.

Why would a random boy appear in the middle of a forest showing me a tree I'm pretty sure wasn't there a minute ago? But she lowered her guard. "Okay. Show me."

She accepted his hand and walked with him. Closer to the tree, she noticed the bright green apples sprayed across its branches.

Bed and breakfast. I like it.

The boy easily scrambled up the trunk to the lowest branch and leaned down, offering his hand again. Etain went to take hold but he pulled it away and shook his head.

"I can't get up there without help."

He pointed at his back and at her.

"My backpack?" It was one thing for her to go with him to the tree but to trust him with her pack and sword? *What if he runs off with them? I'd never catch him.*

As though he knew what she was thinking, he shook his head again, and insisted she pass her pack to him.

In the midst of her personal debate, a twig cracked in the distance. Etain pivoted on her heels, yanked off the cloak and threw it at the boy. While searching the darkness, she ripped off her pack and tossed it to him, backed away a few steps and ran at the tree, scrambling up the branches as far as she could go without compromising her position.

Within seconds, the boy was there and handed over her things.

"Thank you." Settled into her spot with the cloak tucked around her, the plan was to close her eyes for a moment and catch her breath, then spend the evening getting to know her small saviour over a supper of sandwiches and apples.

A cool breeze against her cheek woke her from a deep sleep. Not yet fully conscious, her eyes fluttered as she rolled onto her left side and clasped her hands underneath her chin, drifting back to sleep. To get more comfortable, she shifted her hips but her lower half fell from under her. Wide-eyed, she grabbed at the branches and caught herself, her legs dangling in the air as her backpack fell from the branches to the ground.

What the hell? Why am I in a tree?

She tried to leverage her arms and pull herself up but without much effect.

"Great. I can break a door but can't save myself. Come on, girl. How many trees have you climbed?"

After swinging a leg at a larger branch a couple of times, she managed to get hold and hauled herself back into her leafy haven. Memories from the night before came to her.

"Hello? Little boy?" Etain checked above and below, but there was no sign of the urchin. "At least you gave me a safe place to sleep."

She rolled her cloak into a ball, dropped it to the ground, and plucked a couple of apples from the tree, shoving them into her shirt before shimmying down. "Hasta la vista, my friend. Thank you for watching over me." She slung her pack onto her back, threaded the cloak between the straps, and picked up the apples. "Breakfast."

The first bite filled her mouth with a sweet, tarty juice, making her laugh as she swiped at the dribble down her chin. A sudden movement to her side made her turn. In the underbrush, she spied the light eyes of a black fox watching her. The two stared at one another for a long moment. She enjoyed another bite of the apple and tossed it toward the animal. "Wish I could stick around but I gotta go. Don't let it go to waste."

Etain adjusted her pack and set out toward the gathering she hoped would provide a new future.

<hr />

Well over an hour of listening to birds twitter and sing, she stopped at the sound of human voices. Part of her wanted to rush forward and join the conversation, to be surrounded by others like her hoping to join a clan and learn how to be Alamir.

The other side held her back. *What if they aren't open to someone new?* Her heart raced as she ran a hand through her hair. *What if they're Bok?*

Her breath came in short gasps and her eyes burned. *Don't you cry, Etain.* She swiped away the tears and thought of her brother. *What would Robert do?*

He wouldn't cry.

"No. He'd walk in there like he owned the place."

She pushed the hair from her face, blew out a breath, and took one careful step after another. Hidden behind a tree, she peered into a clearing where five people faced one another.

"RPG much?" she whispered to herself. One girl dressed in brown leather armor had a bow over one shoulder and a quiver of arrows on the other. *Okay, she's not too bad.*

There were two more girls, one dressed in a wannabe Princess Leia bikini and the other was more like an anime character. Etain rolled her eyes. The guys were as diverse, one dressed in the black garb of a ninja, and the other kitted out in impractical armor and a ridiculously huge sword at his side. The garb couldn't possibly be easy to move in.

"Nope. Not my people." She slipped back behind the tree and turned, her plan to take a wide berth around the group and move on by herself.

"Whatcha doing sneaking around? You spying on us?"

Her stomach flipped seeing the boy but kept her cool despite the axe he carried on his shoulder.

Robert's voice sounded in her mind. *Don't ever show 'em you're afraid. Once they get a whiff of fear, it'll be open season.*

She tossed her hair over her shoulder with a shake of her head. "Are you with them?"

With a sneer, he checked her out from head to toe. "I asked first."

Look while you can, Ranger boy. She knew his kind, cocky, too sure of himself, dressed in a long leather tunic over leather trousers and knee-high boots. The axe seemed out of place. But who was she to judge? If he thought it would get him into a clan, so be it.

She glanced at the others from over her shoulder and figured the rest were the same. *Clueless.*

"Are y'all headed to the gathering?"

His lips thinned as he shifted from one hip to the other. "Stop answering my questions with questions."

"Then stop asking." She pivoted in the other direction ready to leave the posers behind.

He grabbed her by the shoulder. Etain stepped back and swung her arm over his head and under his left arm as she shoved her elbow into his chin, forcing his head back. Shifting a leg behind his, she dropped him to the ground in a matter of seconds where he sputtered and gasped.

Etain straightened, pushing her hair away from her face. "You should learn some manners."

Footsteps rustled through the debris of the forest floor.

"Hey, Ranger. You around?"

Etain raised a brow and crossed her arms as he jumped to his feet, dusting himself off. "Wow. *Ranger.* Impressive."

"Shut up." He stepped in front of her. "Hey, guys. What's up?"

Ninja boy stepped from the trees. "Oh, hey." His eyes darted to Etain. "Oh. Uh. Hey. You found another one?"

"Uh, yeah. Another one." Ranger picked up his axe and walked away.

"Okay." Ninja boy turned to Etain and stuck out a hand. "Hi. I'm Clive. Nice to meet you."

Being from Texas, she accepted his hand out of habit. "Hey. I'm Etain. What're y'all doing here?"

"We're on our way to a gathering a couple of towns over."

"Who is we?"

He shrugged. "Uh, that was Ranger."

Etain rolled her eyes. "Yeah. I got that."

"Well, we met each other along the way. Everyone's pretty new." He turned, looking at the group. "The knight is George."

Saint George? Please tell me no. She covered her mouth to hide the smirk.

Clive's brows narrowed but turned back to the others. "He goes by Sir George. You know, after the knight who slayed the dragon."

Etain laughed out loud, unable to hold it back any longer. "That was *Saint* George. And he was never a knight, nor did he slay any dragons."

He scratched his head. "Are you sure? George is pretty adamant—"

"He would be, wouldn't he? Who's gonna challenge him in that get up?"

"Yeah. Okay. So, the girl in the bikini is—"

"Leia?"

His eyes widened. "Do you know her?"

Bless him. He doesn't know any better. "No."

"O-Okay. The rogue is Jinx." He hesitated as though waiting for another comment but Etain had nothing to say.

"The white-haired girl—"

"The anime wannabe with rabbit ears?"

His lips thinned as he breathed in. "She is Kaguya."

Her gaze met his. "Let me guess. You're Naruto?"

A brief smile touched his lips but at the tone of her voice, it disappeared. He changed the subject. "How about you?"

"Yeah, newbie too."

"Really?" He looked her up and down. "Where's your outfit?"

Etain considered it a lame attempt to strike back. She shifted her hips, sticking her hands in her back pockets. "Oh, what, like a teeny-weeny bikini or some Halloween costume?"

He glanced over his shoulder and back at her. "We're doing the best we can."

"Aren't we all?" She walked past him.

"O-Okay. Sorry. You're the only other Alamir I've met outside of these guys."

Etain pulled up, rolled her eyes, and turned to him. "I'm sorry. I forget I'm not the only one. I'm just me. No fancy name or outfit. My jeans and T-shirt do me fine."

He seemed to relax at her confession. "No problem. Why don't you join us?"

"Maybe in a minute. I'm thirsty."

He smiled and twisted, reaching for his pack. "Oh, I got a canteen—"

It was time to go. "It's okay. The river's just over there."

Ninja boy turned his head in the direction she nodded. "Don't take too long. I don't know how safe it is around here."

"Thanks for the warning." She tucked her hands in her front pockets and walked away, hoping he didn't follow.

After several minutes, Etain stopped, listening for sounds of pursuit. When nothing came, she headed to the river and crouched for a sip of the clear, cold water. Voices floated toward her for the second time. She splashed her face and turned toward the line of trees as she stood, shaking her hands dry. The only movement came from the trees swaying in the breeze, but she kept watch as she picked up her pack and shifted it onto her shoulder.

"Maybe it was the wind." To her right, the tops of several buildings showed on the horizon. "It must be the place. Not too far."

At her first step, a scream from the trees stopped her. She resisted her first instinct to run toward the commotion, the same set of "what if" questions running through her head. *What if it's a set-up? What if it's the Bok? Or, what if it's those silly people messing around?*

A second scream followed by several more, both male and female, convinced her that whatever was going on wasn't good. She ran toward the shadows of the trees amidst sounds that didn't belong to a forest—grunts, sobs, and painful moans.

She inched closer to the noises and peeked around a tree. The awkward Ranger lay on his back, blood trickling from the bash on his forehead, surrounded by his unusual travel partners, each of them sporting bruises, cuts, and mud smudges. Several others sat with them, but their injuries appeared a few days older.

Etain counted seven standing guard over the group, three of which were the ugliest creatures she'd ever seen. The three had long, oversized noses drooping over their mouths and tall, pointed ears bent at the ends looking more like skinny wings than ears. Their yellowish-green skin brought to mind a diaper full of baby poo she'd seen once when helping a friend babysit. Then a smell worse than baby poo hit her. She capped a hand over her mouth and turned away, forcing herself to swallow down the bile from her stomach.

What in the hell are those things?

More in control, she edged to the opposite side of the tree. The other four were regular men dressed in brown uniforms, each with a large sword on his hip while the puke monsters carried huge axes.

She turned away again.

Leave it alone, Etain. What're you gonna do on your own?

She leaned around the tree once more and sucked in a breath.

I don't owe them anything.

Whether you do or not, they're Alamir. Where's your loyalty?

She rolled her eyes.

Not much has been shown to me.

Faith, young lady. Perhaps you haven't given them enough time.

And how do you propose I save anyone? Those men are twice my size and fuck knows what those other things are. Their farts'll probably kill us all.

Etain.

I can't save...

She peeked around the tree one last time.

"Goddamn it."

Between the anime girl and Jabba the Hut slave girl sat her small friend from the trees, his knees pulled close to his chest and eyes darting from one face to the other.

Etain untangled the cloak from the backpack, shook it out, and draped it over her shoulders, positioning the hood over her head. "I'm totally gonna regret this."

JUST THE TWO OF US

"You'll regret it if you go in alone." At first, Etain thought it was the voice in her head but realized it wasn't hers.

She glanced over her shoulder giving no indication of her surprise. "What do you know about it?"

A girl with deep blue eyes, dressed in a true Rogue outfit of fitted leathers, leather arm guards, and thigh-high boots, gazed steadily at her. "Do you expect to walk in there and save them on your own?"

Etain figured she wasn't much older than herself. Her Alamir self, not the human. Despite the girl's lovely Southern accent, she didn't trust her. Etain slipped the hood from her head, shifting her weight onto one hip. "I tell you what, why don't *you* go save them while I stand here and watch? Show me how it's done, superhero."

The girl smirked. "I could, but they'd kill most of them before I got close. It's going to take more than just the two of us."

"And you know because?"

She walked toward Etain but her gaze went beyond her. "Those big, ugly things. Do you know what they are?"

Etain turned as she stood next to her. "The smell of them tells me to steer clear."

The girl chuckled. "Clever and correct. Those are goblins, some of the nastiest creatures in the *Bok*. Their drool and blood are like acid. One drop will eat through anything."

Etain sucked in a breath and silently cursed herself for the show of weakness but the girl didn't seem to notice. "Acid?"

"I've never seen one in person, until now. Vivian told me about them."

Etain furrowed her brows giving the girl a cursory glance. "Vivian?"

"Did you think you were the only one?" She smirked. "Silly girl. She's taught *many* others how to fight in the Alamir. Some of the best."

Etain rolled her eyes. "Like you?"

She raised a brow. "Like Jacob."

Etain lowered her eyes and sighed. "Great. I feel like a total ass."

"It's a lot to take in. Don't sweat it. I'm Vix."

"Hey. I guess you know who I am." The girl grinned and nodded. Etain knew the answer to her next question but had to ask, "So, Vix, how long have you been following me?"

"Since you left Vivian."

"I knew I felt something." She ran a hand through her hair. "My senses must be off."

"Well," Vix lowered her head, "if it makes you feel better, I *did* lose your trail last night, couldn't find a trace. Where'd you go?"

"I slept in the big apple tree. I'm pretty sure I left some serious markers in the dirt. It took me a few tries to get into it."

Vix narrowed her eyes and cocked her head. "What apple tree?"

"The biggest one in the forest? If you were behind me, you couldn't have missed it."

"There wasn't an apple tree."

She frowned but remembered her pack and reached inside for a fresh, green apple. "Then where did I get this from?"

Vix grabbed it from her hand and sniffed. "You could've brought it from town." Her eyes widened as she bit into it. "Oh my."

"I assure you I didn't get it from Vivian." Etain shook her head when Vix offered her the apple. "No, you finish it. Once we get those people free, I'll take you back and show you."

A scream made them both turn. One of the brown uniforms had hold of the boy who helped Etain. She reached for her sword, but Vix grabbed her by the arm.

"Whoa! What are you? Twelve? You and your little sword aren't gonna help—"

"No. I'm fourteen." The glare she gave Vix left no room for argument. "I can't sit here and watch them hurt a little boy."

Vix eyed her from head to toe. "Hmph. Fourteen?"

"No shit."

"How long ago?" Vix's attention returned to the goblins.

"A couple of weeks? Months?" She shrugged. "I've lost count. I didn't look like this before I came to the Alamir."

Vix glanced at her. "Does your family know?"

"My family is none of your business."

"Sorry. At this point, it doesn't matter." Vix's gaze returned to group.

"What do we do now, Vix?"

All eyes were on the two of them. Brown uniforms, goblins, and captives. The brown uniforms motioned to the goblins.

"We run." Vix turned away.

Etain grabbed her by the shoulder before she made her move. "We can't outrun those things."

"Then what do you suggest, Ms. Know It All?"

Etain drew her sword and dagger. "We have to fight."

Vix drew her dual short swords. "I'm so going to regret this."

The closer the goblins came, the greater their ugliness grew. Drool dripped down their long chins and their ferocious mud-colored eyes forced Etain back several steps. She collided into Vix, who stepped forward to meet the oncoming threat. At the moment of impact, a bright light flashed.

Etain twisted away and glanced at the girl. "Are you okay?"

Vix wobbled but kept on her feet. "What was that?" Finding her balance, she looked out from where they stood. "How'd we end up over here?"

"What?" Etain turned. Where everyone had faced them before, now their backs were turned. She shared an uneasy glance with Vix. "What're they looking at?"

"At us," Vix snapped. "But we're not there anymore."

"Huh?"

"What did you do, Etain?"

"Me? I ran into you, and boom, we're here. What did *you* do?"

"Whatever either of you did, how about cutting us loose before those assholes realize what's happened?"

Etain turned in the direction of a whispered voice and recognized the Ranger from before.

"Come on!"

The girls ducked and dashed toward the group. "Has anyone seen the little boy?"

A few glanced at one another but shook their heads as Etain passed through them. "He was here. How could no one have seen him?"

The Ranger shrugged. "Sorry. There aren't any little kids with us."

Vix cut off any retort Etain may have had. "Do you know where your weapons are?"

Another young man in jeans and T-shirt pointed toward the other side of the clearing. "They took 'em over there."

"You and the Ranger, get them passed out quick as you can before the—"

"I'll help," the wannabe Princess Leia said.

The three scurried toward the pile and spread out, tossing weapons hand to hand toward the others.

"Hey!" A gruff voice echoed off the trunks of the trees. "Stop them!"

The small group of Alamir swarmed the pile, grabbing whatever weapon they could get their hands on.

Vix caught Etain's eye. "Looks like we're out of time."

Etain breathed in. "I have to find the boy."

"Not that *I* saw one..." Vix sighed. "Where did you see him last?"

"One of the brown uniforms dragged him into those trees over there."

The Ranger returned with axes in both hands. "Go find him. We got this."

Etain checked the others and was glad to see everyone well-armed. She turned to Vix, who nodded in the direction she'd indicated.

"Be mindful of what's around you."

Etain slipped her dagger into her boot, pulled the hood over her head, and picked up her sword. "Be right back."

As the group surged forward toward the oncoming threat, Etain retreated into the trees and moved as quickly as she could to the point where she'd last seen the boy. All she found were more trees and shrubs. No boy, no brown uniform, and nothing to indicate anyone had come this way in quite a long time. The sounds of clashing swords and the grunts of soldiers in combat faded as she worked her way deeper into the forest. She soon realized it was a useless endeavor.

Did I imagine it?

Etain bit her bottom lip as she turned but stumbled back. Her gaze travelled up the long length of the goblin in front of her, a leer in his dreadful eyes, and what she could only surmise as a smirk on his ugly mug. She swallowed and gripped her sword ever harder.

He laughed as he rested his large axe over his shoulder and ran a long, brown tongue over his yellow teeth. She fought to maintain a neutral expression, but the smell of his breath made it impossible.

"Take off the cloak. Let me get a good look at you."

She forced down another swallow to keep from vomiting. "Fuck off."

Her plan was to dash past him and join the others. She could easily outrun this overgrown toad but as she turned, the creep reached behind a tree and dragged the boy out.

"Not much more than a tidbit but tasty enough. Take another step and I will bite off his head."

The boy's lips trembled. Etain recognized the fear in his eyes. Her mouth went dry and her heart thumped so hard she thought she might pass out. "Let him go."

The gravelly laugh crawled over her skin. "Show yourself."

She lifted her head and pulled back the hood with one hand. The goblin seemed to be taken by surprise. The boy must have noticed the momentary hesitation too. He twisted one way and the other and broke free from the goblin's grasp, disappearing into the brush.

Snapped from his stupor, the goblin swung his axe out at Etain. She was far enough away from his reach but still jumped back and raised her sword. Although frightened as hell, she grasped the humor of her situation. Her bitty blade against something four times her size with an even bigger weapon.

I should've run when the kid did.

The goblin moved faster than she expected. As his axe crashed toward her, she dodged. The huge weapon embedded into the ground, but the goblin raised it again with little effort.

This time, she ran forward and cut to her right. He twisted into a turn; the axe handle gripped in both his grubby hands as he swung it round. Etain glanced over her shoulder and realized too late she should've cut to her left. There was no time to get out of the axe's path. Still in motion, she intended to face her fate, but whether it was her own feet or the grass, something tangled between her feet. She fell, her cloak billowing behind her.

For a split-second, she was frozen in mid-air unable to breathe, but the cloak gave way to the might of the blade, and she fell face first. In the next instance, a force of nature dragged her across the ground. She twisted and turned, trying to break free but just as quickly came to a stop.

Etain pushed up on her hands and knees, spitting bits of leaves and dirt, and peered over her shoulder. A large white wolf lunged at another goblin, snatched a small black fox from its clutches, and bolted into the trees.

A male voice yelled, "Grab the silver-hair!"

Silver hair? She glanced around the perimeter, searching for someone with silver hair until it sank into her brain what they meant. Goblins and brown uniforms disengaged from the battle and headed in her direction.

"Holy shit!" She scrambled to her feet, searching for her sword. Unfortunately, it lay a couple of yards away, lost as she was dragged away from the goblin. *Next best thing, then.* She reached for her dagger and held it close at her side, ready to strike at the first one who grabbed at her.

Rather than stand still, she side-stepped, inching her way closer to her sword, her gaze on the grunts stalking toward her. The goblins growled, brandishing their axes, yet she kept moving one step at a time. One pulled ahead of the others, his ugly slit of a mouth curved up at the corners into a salacious grin. He came at her so fast, she stumbled backward and fell on her bottom, staring into the face of her death.

A large green hand reached for her.

From out of nowhere, a large force brushed past her, raising his claymore as he vaulted from the ground and brought it down, slicing through the goblin's forearm.

"Jacob!"

Someone grabbed her from behind and dragged her out of the line of acid fire just as Jacob lopped off its head.

"Get out of here, Etain. We got this." Vivian spun her around.

Her brown leather armor was a surprise but Etain shoved her away. "I can't leave."

Vivian's features hardened. "You are not ready for this."

"How am I gonna learn if—"

She grabbed Etain by both arms and lowered her voice. "You cannot be here. You are too valuable. Follow the map and get to the town. Find Sid and Angel."

With a huff, she leaned back. "Who the hell are they? How am I—"

"They will find you. Go!" Vivian pushed her away.

Rubbing her arms, Etain watched her run back to Jacob "I'm not leaving without my sword," she murmured and jogged the few feet to her weapon. Once in her hand, she glanced across the field. Vivian faced two brown uniforms, holding her own as Jacob took on another goblin. But Etain saw what he could not. From his blind side, the third goblin raced toward the unsuspecting Alamir.

She might not be ready for the fight but there was no way these goons were going to ambush her friend. As she opened her mouth to warn him, the first goblin sneered and hit Jacob with a backhanded slap, knocking him flat on his back. When the goblin lifted her friend over its head, her powers exploded.

Electrical sparks flashed around her body as she lifted her sword. A single bolt of light shot across the field ripping through the goblin in motion and into the one holding Jacob. Both burst into blue flames. Her eyes widened at the havoc but had no idea of how to stop and staggered from the reality of her actions, landing on her butt, horrified by the smoking mess of the two goblins and Jacob.

"I-I..." Tears burned in her eyes. She had to get to him. "Jacob. Jacob!"

Vivian intercepted her within a few steps. "No, Etain! Go! Get out of here."

The tears flowed freely down her cheeks. "But I have to—"

"You can't help him now. Go! Pull yourself together and get to the town. Here's your pack. Please tell me you still have the map."

Etain silently nodded.

Vivian gave her a quick hug and whispered in her ear, "We always rise."

"What?"

She turned her around and shoved her toward the river. "Don't look back. Don't stop. Keep walking until you get to that town. Sid and Angel will find you."

From over her shoulder, Etain watched Vivian run toward the smoldering Jacob. "I'm sorry, Jacob. I'm so sorry." She faced the river, swiped the back of her hand over her face, and took her first steps toward a future she wanted no part of.

A YOUNG WOMAN LEARNS

E tain ran toward the river, determined to keep moving forward. No matter how every fibre of her being ached to do so, she didn't drop to her knees and wallow in her misery. But the tears returned, blurring her vision, and covering her cheeks with their salty residue.

Over and over, the same words repeated in her mind, *I'm sorry. I'm sorry. I'm sorry*, until she puked. She balled her hands into fists, beating her thighs. "I'm no better than the murderer who killed Mom and Dad. How could I be so stupid? I'm a fucking wild card and now I've killed, no, murdered, a good friend. No wonder Vivian told me to leave."

Stretched out on her stomach, she dunked her head into the river. The cold water not only cleansed away the debris from her hair and face, it also brought her one step back toward sanity. After a long drink, she stood but stumbled aimlessly alongside the river wishing she could go home.

"Shut up, Etain! You don't have a home anymore. You could've stayed with Vivian and Jacob. She's probably told this Sid and Angel to take me to..." Her gears switched from the abuse to elsewhere. "What do the Alamir do with people like me? Do I go to jail? Dad never mentioned anything."

She stared at the tree branches swaying in the breeze. "Maybe they'll take me to the Mobius Arena and throw stones at me until I bleed to death. It's what I deserve."

When she turned, a smudge in the distance caught her eye. "Is that a bridge?" She grabbed the map from her back pocket and eyed it again. "It looks to be the same. If I'm lucky, they'll send me back to the human realm. If not, I'll see you soon Mom and Dad."

⋯⋯✦❖✦⋯⋯

Wrapped in her cloak of self-pity and focused on the town nearby, she considered herself to be well out of danger and let down her guard, not paying attention to anything other than the map and her thoughts. The ground tremors did not register, nor did the stench.

"Almost there," she whispered, eyeing the map again, following the river to the bridge.

Within a few feet of the main road, claws dove into her tangled hair, the tips scraping the flesh of her scalp.

"Shit!" The map fell from her hand and her brain exploded with thoughts of what the fuck and who. Whatever ensnared her within its grip was huge and smelly and ripped the pack from her body. *There must've been another goblin. Shit! Shit! Shit!* It pulled her head back as she grabbed hold of the claw in her hair. For a moment, she stared into eyes she would never forget. The red eyes of the assassin.

"There you are," he growled. "I've been looking for you."

His words snapped her out of the momentary funk. Her brother's training flashed in her mind; her moves fluid as though she'd performed them since birth. Knees bent, she turned and punched. With him being a nine-foot-tall demon, she pummelled what was easily accessible without considering if he had a cock and balls. His pants had buttons, so her chances were good. Whether he did or not, his grip loosened, and she twisted away, running toward the river where her pack had landed.

Etain drew her sword and slipped the backpack over her shoulders, her eyes on the demon. *If I'd a seen that face instead of the eyes, I think I would've died where I stood that night.*

Atop his head sat what she considered a man bun of serpents, each one hissing and tiny tongues darting in and out. His scaled turquoise skin had highlights of gold brushed around the eyes and almost nonexistent lips. One eye sported a nasty scar across it, making her wonder if it even worked and his hands consisted of five long spindly fingers tipped by lethal claws. His nose splayed across the middle of his face with large nostrils that spread his foul breath for miles.

Bent on a knee, the demon growled and pushed to his feet with a gruesome laugh. "Nice play, Alamir. But it won't save you. There's a fair price on your little head and I intend to take it."

"I have more need of it than you." She lifted her sword, wishing she didn't have to breath.

"Don't care. You're coming with me." He walked toward her. "I will break you and your prick of a sword in half. As long as you're breathing, I'll get paid."

With the bridge not far away, she moved to her right, hoping to make a run for it. "So, you aren't gonna cut off my head?"

"It would make a tasty meal, sucking out that clever little brain. Better than crawdads." He ran a long black tongue over his gold dusted lips. "But I wouldn't get paid as much. Come here!"

She swiped her sword at his claws and skipped further away. "No way, man. Besides, how do you know I'm the one you're looking for?"

The question made him stop. His eyes turned from red to a marble blue interspersed with gold flecks. Beautiful eyes for a brutal assassin. When his sights returned to her, they turned red. "Your powers. No one in the Alamir has seen anything like it. You are one of a kind and worth a lot of money."

Her heart beat faster. "H-How long have you been tracking me?"

His pointy tooth grin was worse than his black tongue. "Since your show in the first town."

She slid a foot back as she spoke, "What took you so long?"

"My business demands discretion. I can't afford having my face on a poster." He laughed in his horrible way again.

How do I beat this guy? Can I? She considered her sword. Jacob had been an accomplished smithy, but she doubted hers would last long against the monster blade on this demon's back. *Jacob. Fuck. Maybe I should—*

While she was distracted by her thoughts, the demon made his move and grabbed her by the arm. Quick reflexes on her part brought her sword round, stabbing him in the throat. Whether it penetrated his thick skin or not, it certainly pissed him off. A backhanded slap across the face snapped her head back and she almost lost her footing but for his strong grip.

Woozy from the assault, she struggled to keep her wits about her but gave the demon a bloodied grin. "It's funny how the cut matches up to the slit of your eye."

He let go of her. She slumped to the ground on her knees and bent over, touching her forehead to the grass and breathed for several counts, taking a quick inventory of her surroundings.

Pack on back. Good. Sword. Where's my sword? Unaware of what the demon was doing her eyes slid sideways to her right, nothing but sand, grass, and the river, closed her eyes for a moment, and looked to her left. *There you are—just within reach. Good. What's your plan, Stan?*

A dirty, pointy-toed boot blocked her view of the blade. "All the plotting in the world isn't going to get you out of this one."

"Fuck you."

The demon crouched in front of her. "What was that? You want to fuck me?" He chuckled and leaned closer. "I'll be the last fuck you ever have little girl."

Etain came up, throwing a handful of sand into the demon's face, lunged for her sword, and rolled to her feet. Still in a crouch, he shifted onto his back foot, swiping at the sand in his eyes, leaving the other booted foot open. Etain held the hilt with both hands, raised the blade and plunged her blade through the middle of his gargantuan foot.

The demon abandoned the sand in his eyes for the excruciating pain in his foot, yelling words she didn't understand.

Etain yanked the blade free and skipped back a few steps. "Don't be sad. We'll meet again one day and I'll fuck you from head to toe, one slice at a time. Just like you did my family."

A claw clamped onto her ankle. "I'll rip you in half with my cock and sell your bloody cunt to the *Bok*."

Again, she raised her sword but plunged into his arm this time, pinning it to the ground. "Let me go or I'll saw off your hand with my dagger."

He swung out with his other claw, making a play for the knife in her boot. She grabbed it first, but his hold remained firm on her ankle despite the sword through his forearm. He lunged again wrapping his free claw around her throat and squeezed, forcing her into an awkward position.

"I don't care if you're alive or dead," he spat in her face. "I'll fuck you while you're warm and keep fucking until rigor mortis sets in. You should be a nice, tight fuck then."

Rebellious to the end, she quipped, "I doubt even rigor mortis would help in your case," stabbing her dagger into his side several times.

At last, his grip loosened and he collapsed onto his back.

Etain wiped her dagger on his shirt, slipped it into her boot, and moved toward her sword. But the blade rose from the ground still encased in the demon's arm. Eyes wide, she stumbled back, turned, and ran for the bridge.

Coming to the road, she turned to check the demon's position. A gust of wind lifted the ends of her hair just before the world went dark.

The first thing Etain noticed was the quiet around her. No rushing water, no panting goon, no disgusting stink. She opened her eyes. Trees. Everywhere. *Where am I?* As she moved to sit up, she yelped at the pain in her left arm. Nothing made sense, especially the sword through her upper arm. *How'd you get there?*

Upon closer inspection, she realized it was her own sword. Then she remembered the demon, sighed and rolled her eyes. *How'd I get here?*

She searched the forest, listening for telltale signs of a heavy foot or a smelly breath.

Oh. I did this. Again. Damn, I was almost to the town.

Maybe it's best I didn't go that way. He would find me for sure.

So, we start over. I have to go over that bridge to get to the town and I have to go to that town to find Sid and Angel.

What if I stick to the forest past the bridge and come back to it from the other side?

What if I pass out again?

"Well, you don't. You suck it up and keep moving. Who knows how much time has passed."

With the help of a tree, she got to her feet. The sun was low in the western sky. "Maybe I can get there before dark. I hope."

The last town had been smaller, but noisy and active. This one was quiet. She walked along the cobbled road, and although she didn't see anyone, felt like someone was watching her. Stopped in the middle of the road, she turned, her eyes keen for any movement. When nothing came for her, she continued her walk, holding her left arm close to keep it from jarring too much.

How am I supposed to find two people I've never met? How are they gonna know who I am?

She snorted. *The damn demon found me. Why not them too?*

Something whizzed past her left ear, lifting the ends of her hair. She narrowed her eyes and turned. Another buzz passed her right ear but this time she heard it lodge into something nearby. Her eyes darted around the area until she spied an arrow stuck in a wooden door not far from where she stood. *What the hell?*

In the next instant, footsteps were coming her way. Faster and faster. She turned to a boy with a baseball bat running at her. The idea that someone wanted to hit her with a bat struck her as ridiculous. So ridiculous in fact she didn't feel threatened or angry and waited until he was within striking distance before taking a sidestep and watched him run straight into a wall.

She walked toward the unconscious body lying on the ground. "You're gonna have one hell of a bruise. Oop, yeah, it's already showing. Dumbass."

"What've you done to our friend?" a man's voice asked.

"You shouldn't be here, missy," another said.

Great, news travels faster than I thought. "I-I didn't mean to hurt him."

A small group of men and women spanned the width of the road, each one holding a weapon of some sort—bows, swords, a whip or two, and an axe.

"Yeah, well, you're gonna pay for what you did to him."

Between the hammering of her heart and the churning in her stomach, her head spun. "I didn't mean to hurt him. He was my friend too."

A tall, lean man dressed in black leather armor approached. "How do you know Alexander?"

"Who's Alexander?"

He pointed at the unconscious boy. "You said he's your friend."

"I don't know *him*."

"Who are you talking about, then?"

"Jacob."

"Is Jacob the one who stabbed you with that sword? I doubt he's much of a friend."

Etain bit her bottom lip. "He is, was my friend. The sword came later."

A shorter man wearing actual metal armor joined the first. "Fredric, maybe it's why they sent her, thinking she'd scare us into giving in."

Fredric laughed and addressed the group. "Let's show 'em what scared is."

Etain frowned, pivoted on her heels and ran up the road, making a quick right, a left, and another right before she slowed down to catch her breath. She rounded the next corner and stopped, leaning against a wall. The wound stung something awful now.

Running a hand through her hair, she saw a gathering of people in the road. *Dang. They're fast. How could that many get in front of me so quickly?* Then realized it was a different group.

Holy shit.

She inched along the wall hoping for a quick getaway. The clearing of a voice told her she'd run out of luck.

"There she is," Fredric said.

Someone from the other group yelled, "Did ya think us such a bunch of pussies a girl'd scare us into joining your lousy clan?"

The metal-armored man raised his sword. "You're lucky she's a fast runner."

"Were she one of ours, she'd know better than to lead your lame asses straight to us."

"Well, if she isn't yours and she isn't ours..." The tall man gawked at her. "Who the hell are you?"

Etain glanced from one clan to the other and straightened her shoulders as best she could. "I am Etain."

Both clans stared at each other. "Who the hell is Etain?"

"I am."

"I don't know this girl. Hey, Gordo," the tall man yelled across the gap, "do you know who she is?"

Gordo laughed. "Nope and don't care. Your little ploy won't work, Fredric. Prepare to die." The man raised his large sword and ran at them followed by the others.

Etain pressed her body against the wall to get out of the way but found herself engulfed by the two clans, being pushed, and pulled, punched, and grabbed. Every move jarred the sword in her arm. She suffered a few cuts and was certain there would be plenty of bruises. If she survived.

In the next moment, someone from behind made a grab for her sword and pulled it from her arm. She screamed from the pain and slapped a hand over the wound, thinking of a way to staunch the flow of blood. As she whirled around, the thief was off.

"Hey! Come back, you shit!" Etain pushed at the crowd and ran after him, her anger growing with every step. Her first instinct was to raise her hand and zap him with her charge, but the memory of Jacob smoldering in the grass put the urge to rest and distracted her long enough to lose track of the boy. Her shoulders slumped while tears of pain slipped down her cheeks. She bit her bottom lip, curled her one hand into a fist, and closed her eyes. "Damn it! You little shit. I really liked that sword and not just because Jacob made it for me."

This time the memory of her friend pushed her beyond her limits. She collapsed into a blubbering puddle of misery for his loss, the loss of his gift, and for everything else that had happened to her since the death of her family. "I fucking give up. I'm sorry, Daddy."

She crawled into a nearby alcove, ripped the bottom of her T-shirt off, and wrapped it around her upper arm, tying it as best she could. "If I bleed to death by morning, so be it. I'm not a warrior. I can't be Alamir." She shoved the pack onto her lap and curled her body around it, wishing she had her cloak against the chill. The tears didn't stop until she fell asleep.

⁓ ·🙢🙠· ⁓

A hand on her shoulder startled her awake. The morning light burned her swollen eyes and made them water. It would be so easy to cry again. *No more crying. It'll be over soon.*

"Am I going to jail?"

The silver-haired man crouched next to her. His beard matched his hair and set off his blue eyes. "Why would I do something stupid like that?"

His southern drawl lowered her anxiety level a titch, but she scowled. "Because I was stupid."

He raised a silver brow. "Like lose your blade and cloak?"

She ducked her head, resting her forehead against her pack. "What's it to you?"

"Well," he leaned back on his heels, "I found this little candy sticker." He drew a sword from the pack on his back.

Etain sat up straight. "How'd you get…" Her eyes met his. "How do you know it's mine?"

"We've been waiting for you." She hadn't noticed the blond woman dressed in blue leather armor standing behind him until she spoke. "I'm Angel. This here's Sid. Vivian told us what happened. Here..." she held out a dark cloak, "let's get this on you."

Etain snorted. "Great. What happens to me now? You gonna take me to the Mobius Arena and kick my ass?" She slipped her blade into the side of her pack.

Sid laughed as he rose to his feet. "Girl, you got some imagination, talking about jail and the Arena. What's gotten into you?"

She glared at the man and shoved her pack at him, forcing him back a few steps, and pushed to her feet. "Jacob's dead because of me!"

Angel placed a hand on Sid's forearm and stepped past him. "Jacob's fine." She laid the warm fabric over Etain's shoulders. "But it doesn't look like you are. What's happened here?" She pointed at her bandaged arm.

"Never mind that. I saw him burn." She gladly accepted the cloak but thought, *She must be lying.*

"Child, fire is the last thing to hurt that man. There's a reason why he's a smithy."

Sid crossed his arms over his chest. "And a damn good one too."

Etain stared at the two. "What?"

Angel gently took her hand in hers. "Jacob is alive, Etain."

Oh, how the simmering tears burned. "How?"

"Sid, maybe you should tell her while I have a look at her arm." Angel gently unfastened the material and unwrapped it.

He stroked his beard and smiled. "Vivian told us about your power. A blue electric thingy?" His description of her power brought a slight smile to her lips. "We haven't seen it but it sounds incredible. Well, Jacob's power is fire. He said your little light show took him by surprise, but he was damn happy to see it. Otherwise, he'd been fried by the Goblin's acid."

Etain almost laughed. "You actually talked to him?"

He tapped his ear and showed her the earpiece. "Yep."

She wanted to laugh and cry and shout her relief. "So, if I'm not going to jail or the Arena, where *are* we going?"

Sid picked up her pack. "We're gonna introduce you to G."

She grabbed it from his hands and stepped back. "Wait a minute. How do I know you're who you say you are?"

He glanced at Angel and shrugged. "How else would we know your name or where you came from?"

Etain eyed one and the other. "I said my name back there." She cocked her head in the general direction she'd come from. "I also mentioned Jacob. Maybe you were part of the clan bash and saw me walk into town. You would've seen my sword." She lifted her arm to show them the wound. "Maybe this is some screwed-up plan to lure me to—"

Sid shifted on his feet. "Where? For what reason?"

"How the hell do I know? To this G person." She waved the injured arm in the air and noticed there was no wound. No blood. Not even a mark. She touched her arm and looked at the woman. "What did you do?"

Angel shrugged. "There was blood on the cloth. I thought you were injured."

"I was. Are you a healer?"

"I've helped a few in my day but me, no, I'm not a healer. What happened?"

"Nothing of consequence. I've always healed quickly." *But not like this.* Etain slipped her pack onto her back anxious to get as far away from these people as possible. Maybe Vivian and Jacob as well as these two weren't so nice. *She had to have done something when I was talking to him.*

"Look," Sid swiped a hand over his face, "we didn't know you were here until I saw some little cockroach running down the street with that toothpick you call a sword. Jacob has a very distinctive style. I've seen his work plenty of times." He shifted again, placing his hands on his hips. "And he doesn't smithy swords for just anyone."

"Oh," she said contritely and admitted to herself that she didn't necessarily feel threatened or scared. It was more a matter of being thorough and not making another stupid mistake.

"Calm down, Sid. You can't blame her for being cautious." Angel turned to Etain. "G is the chieftain of the Darth clan. Our clan. To be completely honest, we've been searching for you since your show in St. Clears. And after what happened with Jacob, I'm certain G is one of the few people who can teach you how to control it."

Etain ran a hand through her hair as she considered what had been said. "You think he can?"

"There's only one way to find out." Angel smiled. "Are you with us?"

ALSO BY

INTO THE KAOS TRILOGY
CROSSFIRE
KEY OF G
ONCE UPON A DARKNIGHT

THE BLOOD OF KAOS SERIES
ALAMIR
DREAMREAPER
FLESH AND BONE
TABOO

NOTE FROM NESA

Thank you for reading my book(s)!
Whether you love them or hate them,
please share your experience with other readers
and tell them of your journey Into the Kaos.

ABOUT THE AUTHOR

After marrying her special someone, Nesa decided life was too short to spend it all in one place. Instead of him moving to Texas (her home), she moved to England (his home). Since then, life has been an adventure!

Nesa is a 'learn as you go' kind of gal, which can be challenging, especially when it comes to writing. Although it took a backseat to raising her three children and work, the desire to write never died. Now that her kids are grown, she can indulge in her fantastical stories.

You can find Nesa Miller here:
https://ladyofkaos.com/
FACEBOOK – Nesa Miller
AMAZON – Nesa Miller
TIKTOK – Lady of Kaos

ACKNOWLEDGEMENTS

A SPECIAL THANK YOU TO

Daniel, my incredible husband – I adore you!

Amy Briggs – Editor Extraordinaire

Amy Queau – Q Designs – Cover Artiste Magnifique

Daniel Palfrey – Talented Artiste

Jennifer Khan – Sassy SEO Marketeuer

CAN I JUST SAY

Many years ago, a small group came together
in the spirit of community.
They called themselves superheroes.
Super they were and super they remain.
Thank you for your super ways, support,
and continued friendships.

Long live all you Superdudes!